D0720380

Note to Readers

While the Lankford and Miller families are fictitious, their journey from Boston to Cincinnati mirrors the experiences of hundreds of families during the early 1800s. When the British, who were fighting against Napoleon in Europe, began kidnapping American sailors and illegally forcing them to work on British warships, President Jefferson ordered all American ports on the East Coast closed.

As a result of this action, merchants, shipbuilders, and the businesses who provided supplies for them went out of business. Rather than go through years of unemployment, many families moved to Pittsburgh, Cincinnati, and other growing cities in the interior of America to start new lives. While some of the young Americans who had been captured by the British managed to escape and some were eventually released, many others simply disappeared and their families never learned what happened to them.

ADVENTURE
in the
WILDERNESS

Veda Boyd Jones

BARBOUR
PUBLISHING, INC.
Uhrichsville, Ohio

For my three sons—Marshall, Morgan, and Landon—
with love

© MCMXCVII by Barbour Publishing, Inc.

ISBN 1-57748-230-1

All rights reserved. No part of this publication may be reproduced or transmitted in any form or by any means without written permission of the publisher.

Published by Barbour Publishing, Inc.
P.O. Box 719
Uhrichsville, Ohio 44683
http://www.barbourbooks.com

Member of the
Evangelical Christian
Publishers Association

Printed in the United States of America.

Cover illustration by Peter Pagano
Inside illustrations by Adam Wallenta.

CHAPTER ONE
The Plan

"Cincinnati!" Betsy Miller wailed to her friend Mary. "It might as well be the moon."

"As if someone could go there," Mary said with a sniff.

The two girls huddled in heavy cloaks on their favorite pier at Boston Harbor and watched the waves. A few boats bobbed on the water a mile or so out.

"Father says a frontier town like Cincinnati could use a doctor, but I don't think that's the reason we're going. I think it's because Uncle Paul wants to go, and he's talked Father into it. With the embargo, there isn't much shipbuilding going on, and he needs work."

Betsy glanced down the wharf. The shipyard where Paul Lankford had worked was unnaturally silent. The cold sea wind whipped her hair into her eyes, and she pushed back the brown curly locks. She wrinkled her nose at the fishy smell on the brisk breeze.

"But why Cincinnati?" Mary asked. "I thought Pittsburgh was where riverboats were built."

"I don't know why. All they said was we were going as soon as arrangements were final. They've been planning this for months, but they just told me. And, of course, George is going." Of all her relatives, George Lankford was her least favorite. He was only eleven, two years her junior, but he was a good foot shorter than she was, and he never let her forget that she was extremely tall for a girl.

"How's the weather up there?" he'd ask every time she saw him, which was frequently since their parents were close friends as well as cousins.

The teasing was one thing, but he was also her exact opposite. Where she was shy, he was outgoing and impatient with her reluctance to speak or act upon a situation until she had studied it. Answering the teacher's questions in school dismayed her, but George would wave his hand to get the teacher's attention.

It had taken her two years to become good friends with Mary, and now she was being jerked out of a comfortable situation and thrown into a new place where she'd know no one. She'd have to make new friends. George told her it would be a great adventure. Betsy thought of it as torture.

"Do you think you'll see wild Indians?" Mary asked.

"I fear we will. Probably we'll be scalped before we reach Ohio," Betsy said with a shudder. "I don't want to go. I don't want to be constantly badgered by George. He delights in embarrassing me."

Betsy shook her head, remembering the time George had taken her lunch pail and put it on the shelf at the front of the schoolroom. He'd had to move a chair over and climb up, but she had easily reached it from her standing height. The other students had watched her face turn as red as a burning hot coal. They'd laughed, and she'd grabbed her pail and run back to her desk. She'd sat staring down at her desk while school went on around her.

"What you ought to do is get him back. Embarrass him," Mary suggested. "Let's go over to my house. It's getting colder."

Betsy nodded and got to her feet, but she still looked out at the water. It was probably useless, this vigil she kept of going to the pier every day to look out toward the sea. Her cousin Richard was an American sailor who had been kidnapped and forced into naval service by the British over a year ago. It was unlikely that he would be released while the Napoleonic War still raged, because the British needed good sailors like Richard. Hundreds of American young men had been impressed, as they called it. Their families had no idea where they were or if they still lived.

Betsy felt powerless to help Richard, but going to the harbor made her feel closer to the older cousin who had always been kind to her and who had taught her to play the violin. Her gaze swept the harbor one final time, then she turned away from the water.

The girls trudged to Mary's one-story frame house and sat by the fireplace with their hands and feet stretched out toward the warming flames. Betsy had suggested they meet at the pier since it was where the girls had spent many hours talking in the summer, confiding in each other and watching the ships. It seemed fitting that she break the news of the move there where they could be alone.

Now she heard the clatter of dishes as Mrs. Stover worked in the kitchen. In one corner of the big room, Mary's younger brothers argued over some wooden blocks. The baby cooed in a cradle near the fire. Mary rocked the cradle with her foot as they talked.

"What did you mean about getting even with George?" Betsy asked.

"I don't know. Do things to him like he's doing to you."

"It's not possible to embarrass George Lankford. Besides, he's not short for his age; I'm just tall for mine." At five-foot nine, she towered over everyone in the school. Only one eighth grade boy came close, and he was a half-inch shorter. Her mother told her that she was having her growth spurt early and the others would catch up, but that wasn't much solace now.

"You wouldn't tease him about his height. You'd have to pick something that bothers him."

Something that bothered him. That would take some thinking.

"You could play all kinds of tricks on him on the trip," Mary said. "But you have to promise to write and tell me all about them."

"Promise," Betsy said, looking down at her hands. This had possibilities, but something kept niggling at her mind, resisting the plan. "This wouldn't be the Christian thing to do, would it, Mary? Pastor would say it was wrong."

"Isn't it wrong what George is doing to you?" Mary argued. "If he does unto others as he wants them to do unto him, then he wants to be teased."

"I suppose you're right, although that seems a little backward. Still, I ought to teach him a lesson so he'll stop this. Mother says if you do something over and over, it gets to be the normal thing for you to do, even if it's something bad. If I don't stop George from teasing, he'll be doing it to everybody."

"Exactly."

But what could she do to him? Betsy pondered while she walked home in the shivering cold. A cloud blanketed the sun, and the late Saturday afternoon seemed dismal, matching her mood.

She opened her front door to be met by none other than the object of her thoughts.

"Hey, Betsy," George called with his head tilted back and his hands cupped around his mouth. "How's the weather up there?"

She ignored him. After all, what reply could she give that wouldn't call even more attention to herself? As it was, the grownups in the parlor were all staring at her. Her parents, George's folks, and Richard's mother and father had stopped talking.

"Betsy, I'm glad you're back," her mother said. "We're discussing the move." Betsy had always wondered how her petite mother had married such a tall man. Betsy's father, Dr.

Thomas Miller, measured in at six feet, three inches, and she figured she must have taken after him. He was an awesome figure of a man, one who commanded respect.

He now spoke in a deep baritone voice. "We've booked passage on the schooner Columbia from Boston Harbor and up the Delaware River to Philadelphia. We'll depart Wednesday, March fourth. At Philadelphia we'll ship our belongings on freight wagons to Pittsburgh. Then we'll take the stagecoach."

George's father continued their itinerary. "We'll work together to build a large flatboat at Pittsburgh. I've heard there are many shysters who sell boats that use inferior wood or who don't caulk the joints correctly. We'll be using that wood to build our houses, and we want the best." His recitation sounded as if it were his side of a discussion that had been held earlier.

"We may be in Pittsburgh several weeks while we build the boat," Father continued. "Then we'll float down the Ohio River to Cincinnati. That shouldn't take but a couple of weeks, since it's all downstream. By the time we get there, school will not be in session, but Mother will help you with lessons, and you can start again in the fall in a new school."

He looked kindly at Betsy as if he knew how important school and books were to her. There had been times when she had thought of them as her only friends. Of course she had a copy of the Bible, which she had read cover to cover. She also had copies of four of Shakespeare's plays and a slim volume of poetry.

"I understand there's a library in Cincinnati," Mother added.

That surprised Betsy. She had thought there would be Indians. A library was a civilizing touch to a frontier area she considered beyond the outskirts of the United States. Oh, she knew Ohio was a state in the new country, but that didn't mean it was a place she wanted to go.

"I'm sure it will be fine," she said. It wasn't as if her opinion really mattered. The adults must have made all the plans months ago, but she'd only been told about it the night before. She noticed the papers Father held. He'd probably gotten the tickets. March 4. In a week and a half, they'd be on their way to Cincinnati.

Uncle Charles and Aunt Martha, her cousin Richard's parents, were staying in Boston. They would keep vigil until their son was released from the illegal British impressment or they found out what had happened to him. And they would be in Boston to welcome him home should he return from the war. Betsy tried to push that worry from her mind.

"It'll be great," George said. "Jefferson and I are going to fight Indians."

"The Indians are friendly," Father assured the boy.

"Jefferson is moving, too?" Betsy asked in alarm. She couldn't stand George's dog. Because George was named after the first president, he'd named his dog after the current president, Thomas Jefferson. George had wanted to name the dog Thomas, but Betsy's father didn't like the idea of sharing his first name with a pup. So George had settled for Jefferson.

"You can't think I'd leave Jefferson behind," George said as he jumped, trying to touch the top of the door frame that led into the kitchen.

Betsy sighed in disgust. Now she'd have to put up with that dog as well as with George. She didn't know which was worse. The dog always sniffed around her heels, calling attention to her. But then, George delighted in making her the center of attention, too. Those two belonged together. And she was going to get them both.

Mary's suggestion that Betsy get even with George was sounding better and better. In the next ten days before her family left Boston for good, she and Mary would have to map out the plan.

The next few days flew by. Betsy continued to go to school, but in the evenings, she helped her mother pack.

"We can't take everything with us," Mother said. "We're going to let Pastor have this bed. His family's growing by leaps and bounds."

"This is my bed," Betsy said. "What will I sleep on?"

"We'll get something else in Cincinnati. We'll take the big bed because my grandfather brought it from England. It was my mother's, and she gave it to me."

They sold some of their belongings, gave other things away, and the rest they packed in wooden crates and trunks.

The day before departure arrived. Betsy and Mary, arm in arm, walked home from school.

"Have you come up with any ways to get George?" Betsy asked.

Mary grinned mischievously. "We have to stop by my house, then I'll walk you home." When they reached her home, she ran inside, then reappeared a minute later with a cloth-wrapped package. She held it out to Betsy.

"What's this?"

"Smell it," Mary said.

Betsy unwrapped the bundle. Her nose wrinkled before she could rewrap it. "Whoo! What is this?"

"Limburger cheese. I got it from a peddler on Beacon Street. If you unwrap it and put it with George's clothes, they'll all smell terrible." She laughed.

"How will that embarrass him?"

"Nobody will want to be around him. He always wants to be the center of attention, and that will take care of that."

Betsy nodded and stuck it in her empty lunch pail. She could still smell the stuff. That would get George. "Thanks. Got any other ideas?"

"You'll have to come up with them as you go. Who knows what will happen on your trip? I wish I were going with you."

"Me, too." They had reached Betsy's house, and they stood in the cold wind. Betsy didn't know how to say good-bye to her friend.

"I have a secret," Mary said. "Promise you won't tell."

"Who could I tell? I'm leaving."

"The embargo President Jefferson declared makes Father angry. I heard him tell Mother that the store will go out of business if he doesn't get some goods from England to sell, and that's not going to happen as long as the ports stay closed. He said there were opportunities on the frontier. He mentioned Ohio."

"Do you think you'll move west?" Betsy whispered in awe. Could it really happen? Would her best friend move to Cincinnati, too?

"I don't know. But don't be surprised if someday I knock

on your door and say 'Remember me?' Wouldn't that be something?"

"Mary, that would be the grandest thing. Once we get settled, I'll go to the river every day and look at the boats and pray that you're on one of them." In a way it would take the place of going to the harbor to look for Richard.

The two girls hugged, and then Betsy hurried inside the empty house. Their belongings had been taken to the schooner earlier that day, and all that was left was bedding.

After a sleepless night spent on the floor, Betsy and her parents arose at dawn and made last-minute preparations for the trip. Betsy carried blankets, Richard's violin, and her lunch pail, which secreted the awful-smelling cheese.

"I have a surprise," Father said. As they walked toward the dock, he paused at the livery stable. "I've decided to take Silverstreak with us. If George can have Jefferson on board, surely we can take our mare."

Betsy hugged him. "Oh, Father. I hadn't even hoped that we could take Silverstreak. I couldn't bring myself to tell her good-bye." Together they went inside the stable and bridled the horse. Mary, books, the violin, and Silverstreak were all Betsy's dearest friends. She was taking three of them with her, and maybe Mary would show up someday, too.

Betsy shifted her load of blankets to the mare's back, and they walked on toward the *Columbia*. The clomp of Silverstreak's hooves on the planks of the dock was a reassuring sound to Betsy. She led the horse onto the ship and to the special roped-off section one of the crew showed her. She was tying the mare to a pole when she heard George's voice behind her.

"We won't have to send a sailor up the mast. We'll just ask you when you sight land again," he said.

She ignored him.

"You bringing that horse?" he asked.

She glanced at him. "Of course. Father will need her when he makes calls on patients."

Jefferson ran up to Betsy and sniffed her feet. The small brown dog came upon the pail she had set down and shied away from it, backing right into Silverstreak's makeshift stall. The horse reared; the dog yelped and ran to George.

"Keep your horse away from my dog," George said.

"Keep your dog away from my horse," Betsy said.

A tight smile crossed Betsy's face, and she glanced at the lunch pail that held the stinky cheese. This trip just might be fun.

Chapter Two
The Journey Begins

Betsy stood at the rail and watched the sailors on the wharf make last-minute preparations to cast off. Lines were tossed to sailors in longboats who strained as they rowed, pulling the ship out to sea. Betsy and George had been warned to stay out of the way of the crew, who were scurrying between the two masts readying the sails. Betsy had counted twenty-three other passengers, but none of them were children.

Betsy's mother came up behind them. "Did you put the blankets in the stateroom?"

"Yes, Mother." Betsy had already been below deck to her family's small stateroom. Although the schooner line that ran the regular route between Boston and Philadelphia advertised the accommodations as elegant, Betsy would have argued with that description. It was a stark room that smelled bad, but they wouldn't be on the boat for long. She wished they were already in Philadelphia, and she wished they weren't going at all.

"It will be a better life," her mother said, as if to herself.

"Mother?" Betsy glanced down and saw tears in her mother's eyes. Didn't she want to go, either?

Mother took a deep breath and lifted a hand in farewell to Uncle Charles and Aunt Martha, who stood on the dock. As the ship shifted beneath them, Mother said, "We are leaving your brothers here."

"Oh, Mother." Betsy's three stillborn brothers had been buried in the churchyard. Many times she had wondered what her life would be like if her brothers had lived. The house wouldn't have been as quiet, of that she was sure. It would have been more like Mary's house with constant activity and noise. Betsy hugged her mother's petite frame.

"I know their spirits are with God," Mother whispered. "But this is hard."

Betsy swallowed back tears, but a few found their way down her cheeks. She'd tried to be strong about this move, but now that her mother had let her emotions show, Betsy couldn't hold her tears at bay.

"Is it raining up there? On our big day?"

Betsy stared hard at George, who looked as if he was uncomfortable with all the crying. She almost felt sorry for him. Even though he had referred to her height again, he sounded as if he were trying to cajole her out of her sadness. Maybe she should reconsider her plan of getting back at him.

"Hey, Jefferson." George reached down to pet his dog, who was tied to a pole.

Mother dried her tears with her lace-edged handkerchief and then handed it to Betsy. "George is right. Today is no day for tears. We're starting a new adventure, Betsy. And we should start it with glad hearts." Mother kissed her and moved down the rail to stand by Father.

Betsy gazed back at the wharf and at Richard's folks, who were growing smaller by the minute as the schooner moved away from shore. They had always been kind to her, just like their son. When Richard had first gone to sea, he'd entrusted his prized violin to Betsy's keeping, telling her to keep practicing while he was gone. She'd offered it back to his parents when she found out about her move to Cincinnati, but they'd both said Richard had wanted her to keep playing.

"When Richard returns, he can travel to Cincinnati to get it back," Aunt Martha had said. "Maybe we'll come with him."

She'd said "when" Richard returned, not "if" he returned. Betsy wanted to have the same faith that Richard would return from this war that shouldn't even involve their country.

Jefferson tugged on the hem of her skirt, and she looked

away from the receding shore and toward the pesky dog. "Keep that dog away from me."

George jerked at the line that held the dog, and Jefferson yelped. Curious sailors glanced their way as they adjusted the sails that had caught the wind. They spared a quick look at George, but seemed to study Betsy. She just knew they were staring at her because she was so tall.

"I'm going below," she told George and stepped carefully across the deck toward the steep stairs that led to the staterooms. Once in the safety of her room, she picked up the violin case and drew out the lovely instrument and the bow. She finished one slow, melancholy song that fit how she was feeling, then forced herself to strike up a bright tune to lift her mood.

Mother was right. She should look on this move as an adventure. Once she had hit the last quick note, she put away her violin with a new resolve and made her way to the top deck to check on Silverstreak. She'd heard some animals didn't take to the motion of the boat, and she hoped the mare wasn't suffering any pangs. Certainly motion sickness hadn't affected Jefferson.

Cold wind whipped at her hair and pushed her long skirt against her legs as she crossed from the stairwell opening toward the makeshift stall. Now that they had left the bay, wind that had been blocked by land filled the sails, and the ship cut a sharp line through the water.

"Betsy!"

She turned and sidestepped just in time to avoid being hit by George as he swung on a rope that dangled from a crosspiece on the mast. He swayed back and forth like a pendulum and let out a loud whoop.

"You rapscallion!" a sailor yelled. "Let go of that line!"

"George, what are you doing?" Betsy grabbed the rope to stop the motion, while George held tightly to the end. "You'll cause a shipwreck!"

George dropped to the deck with a thud. "I was just seeing if I could swing. I didn't hurt anything."

"Don't touch these lines," the sailor ordered. Betsy grabbed George by the arm and dragged him along with her toward Silverstreak's stall. Her face burned from the confrontation, even though she wasn't the one who'd done something wrong. "We're going to be on this ship for four days. You'd better stay out of trouble."

George edged around the stall and took a defensive stance, feet shoulder-width apart, head cocked back. "I was just looking around. I'm not hurting anything. Swinging on that rope wasn't going to cause a wreck. The worst it could do was move the sail, and it didn't. I tugged on the rope before I put my weight on it."

"Just be sure you don't cause any more alarm for those sailors. They already have their eyes on us. Father said to stay out of their way."

Betsy turned her attention to Silverstreak and stroked the horse's mane. The animal seemed to be taking the swaying motion of the ship without a problem. When Betsy looked back over her shoulder for George, he was gone. She shouldn't have to worry about him. Where were his parents anyway? She ducked around barrels and poles, until she located her folks and George's. They were standing by the rail looking toward home. Betsy looked past them at the shoreline, which was barely a brown spot on the horizon.

If her second brother had lived, he would have been George's age. For the second time that day she wondered what her life would have been like if he had lived. Surely he wouldn't have been the rambunctious type like George, whose curiosity and eagerness were always making him the center of attention.

Seagulls cawed overhead. Betsy glanced up and watched them circle and occasionally dive in the water in search of fish. She pulled her cloak more tightly around her shoulders and found an unoccupied spot in the sun where she could sit with her back braced against a wooden box that also blocked the brisk wind. The sun felt warm as she watched the seascape. Waves broke against the ship and sprayed a fine mist on the edge of the deck but didn't reach her. Time passed slowly, and she felt herself slipping back into that melancholy mood again.

Betsy must have dozed off, for the next thing she knew, she was in the shade and the chill of March had settled inside her. The sun was higher in the sky than before, but they had changed directions. Father had told her they would tack many times or they would go too far out to sea. She couldn't see any shoreline now, but knew it couldn't be too many miles away. In her secluded spot, she could watch the activity of the sailors and study the passengers who were huddled in small groups here and there. The cold sent her down below, and she found her mother tidying their room.

"I was about to search for you, although it wouldn't take long to find you on a ship this size. Are you feeling better now?"

"Yes, Mother. And you?"

"I'm fine. Sometimes we have to let our feelings out so that we can move forward in life. I'm anxious to get settled in Cincinnati. Your father says it will hold many opportunities for us."

"Yes, Mother," Betsy said, although she had no idea what those opportunities would be.

"Did you pack something in your lunch pail for us? Our passage includes our meals, but I'm wondering how good the cook is." Her mother held the pail that secreted the stinky cheese, and Betsy quickly shook her head.

"No, I'll take that. Shall we join the others?" she asked in an effort to change the subject. They walked into the main cabin, which was dominated by a long table. Quiet conversations buzzed as the passengers ate the meal of stew and hard bread. George sat on the floor with some strangers at the far end of the room, which Betsy guessed was some thirty feet long. She ate quickly, then returned to the stateroom with her mother.

"I had this trunk brought in here instead of stored with the others below," her mother said. "We might have use for it."

Betsy recognized the trunk and quickly unbuckled the straps. Inside, wrapped in clothes for safekeeping, she found her beloved books. *Macbeth* was on top, so she pulled it out, deciding she'd have lots of time for reading while they traveled to Philadelphia. The afternoon passed with her curled up in a dim corner, pouring over the volume.

The next day passed while Betsy alternated between reading and sitting in the sun on the deck, watching the sky and the seagulls and the waves. Occasionally she'd catch a glimpse of land before the ship tacked and headed back to the open sea. Her father assured her the zigzag course was the straightest way the ship could travel south. George stayed out of her sight, and she decided to give up her plan of making him miserable. If he continued to avoid her, they'd get along just fine.

On the third day, the sun failed to peek out behind heavy clouds and the wind howled around the sails. By midmorning, snow fell heavily, disappearing into the water but piling up on deck. Betsy helped Father cover Silverstreak's stall with canvas to protect the horse. After that, the snow made the deck treacherous to walk on, so she merely stuck her head out from below deck to check on the horse.

Even with fewer sails up in an effort to control the ship's motion, many of the passengers got sick from the constant tossing of the ship. Betsy's mother and George's parents suffered seasickness, and Betsy stayed in the tiny stateroom to care for them. The ship sailed out of the storm by late afternoon, but that night few passengers sat at the long table.

Betsy coaxed weak tea down her patients' throats, and her father decided they would all sleep in the one room for warmth and so he could also help with the sick. Before bedtime, Betsy, her father, and George prayed for the recovery of the patients and for a safe journey's end. Betsy changed into her nightdress behind a curtain, laid down beside her mother, and pulled heavy quilts over them. George curled up in the corner with his dog.

After a restful night, Betsy awoke and reached for her

traveling dress. It wasn't lying on the trunk where she had left it. A quick glance around revealed Jefferson curled up in it. "Give me my dress," she whispered, careful not to wake up the others. She and her mother had sewn the dress specially for the trip, and now that dog had shed hair all over it. She jerked on it, and Jefferson gave it up with a sharp bark. Betsy stared at it in horror. The hem of her brand new dress was in tatters where the dog had chewed on it in the night. She couldn't contain a squeal of anger.

"What is it, dear?" her mother asked in a voice that showed she was recovering.

"Jefferson has ruined my dress," Betsy said in a low tone.

"It wasn't his fault," George said. "He got cold in the night, so I covered him with it."

"Then it's your fault," Betsy said, turning on him.

"Let me see it," Mother said. She studied the torn places. "You can turn up the hem and conceal the holes. My sewing kit is in that trunk." Betsy rummaged in the trunk for the necessary items, while George and Father helped the patients into the main cabin for morning tea. Betsy turned up her hem three inches and stitched it, all the while plotting revenge on George and his dog.

She put on the dress and wished she had a looking glass, although she had a good idea what she looked like. In a few hours they would dock in the biggest city in the United States, and she would look like a tall gangly girl in a dress that she'd outgrown.

Once again George had managed to embarrass her. But it would be the last time. Somehow she had to get even. She'd teach him a lesson he needed to learn. She'd even the score.

CHAPTER THREE
Betsy's First Chance

As the ship made its way up the Delaware River, Betsy marveled at the city around her. Almost fifty thousand people lived in Philadelphia, and it looked as if half of them were on the docks. Other ships were loading and unloading. They had already passed three ships that were headed out to sea or maybe up to Boston, she thought longingly for a moment before thoughts of this huge city pushed her old home out of her mind.

Other passengers crowded the deck as they watched the city landscape pass by. Even Mother was topside. Although the afternoon wind was still freezing cold, the sea had calmed down, and Mother said the brisk air made her feel better.

"Betsy, as soon as we dock, take Silverstreak off and to the end of the wharf out of harm's way," Father said. "Keep George with you. Your Uncle Paul and Aunt Eleanor are still under the weather, and it'll take all their strength to make sure their belongings are unloaded and kept together without having to keep an eye on George as well."

Betsy nodded. She didn't want to leave the deck, but she slipped downstairs and got her violin and her lunch pail, then returned to watch the sailors skillfully maneuver the ship into port.

"George, stay with me," she ordered.

George's eyes shown with excitement, or maybe it was mischief she saw in his bright eyes, Betsy decided. As soon as the gangplank was in place, she untethered Silverstreak and led her off the ship. George held on to a rope he had tied around Jefferson's neck. The dog ran ahead as far as the eight-foot rope allowed.

They clomped across the wooden planks and onto the cobblestone street at the end of the wharf.

"Wait here," Betsy said.

"Look, black people," George said and pointed at a group gathered around a barrel.

"Pepper Pot, smoking hot!" They hawked their wares.

26

"Here, hold Jefferson a minute. I want to see what they're selling."

George flung the rope into Betsy's hand before she had time to object, not that he would have listened. He rushed off toward the black people.

Betsy had seen a black person once in Boston, but not up close. Through lowered lashes, she watched the encounter between George and the street sellers. They were talking to him, asking him questions, or was it the other way around?

She tied Silverstreak to a hitching post and was in the process of tying Jefferson to the same post when a wagon drawn by a pair of horses clopped by. One moment she held the dog's rope in her hand, and the next moment he was gone, barking and chasing the wagon. Riding at the back of the wagon was another dog.

"George!" Betsy yelled as she ran after the wagon. Who would have thought a wagon could travel so fast over the uneven cobblestones? Betsy splashed through a puddle where some of the stones had sunk. She glanced back to see that George was running behind her.

The wagon stopped farther along the wharf next to a pile of empty crates, and the driver hopped down and loaded a couple chests. Jefferson barked and climbed the pile of crates so that he was level with the other dog. One crate toppled as Jefferson climbed to another. His bark turned to a whine.

"Come down, Jefferson," George called a second before he climbed on a low crate. He reached for another one, but it teetered a moment, then fell.

"George, don't go up there," Betsy cried. "You'll fall. They can't hold you."

"How am I going to get Jefferson?" George retorted and edged toward another crate.

Jefferson was standing on a high crate, not moving. He seemed frozen in fear. The driver of the wagon had returned to his high seat and yelled, "Giddyup." The horses responded, and the wagon lurched away, with the dog barking a farewell at Jefferson.

Jefferson didn't bark back. He looked at George and put a paw out to move toward him, which dislodged another empty crate. It crashed to the ground, barely missing George, who still clung to his spot in the pile.

It served them both right, Betsy thought. George shouldn't have run off, leaving Jefferson with her, and Jefferson was turning out to be as impetuous as his owner. She stepped back and assessed the situation. Was this her chance at getting back at the dog for chewing her dress? And at George for embarrassing her all those times?

No, this was a matter of the two of them getting hurt. It wasn't the same thing. Besides, Father had told her to watch after George, and she'd better fulfill that responsibility. She pushed a fallen crate over beside George.

"Step here, George, and climb down. If we build a couple steps, you should be able to get your dog."

George shot her a grateful look, then followed her order. Once he was safely on the ground, he helped Betsy push a crate right below the area where Jefferson hovered, and she held it stable while George climbed on it.

It wasn't enough. Betsy found another crate that could be moved without bringing the whole pile down.

"I'll sit on the bottom crate and hold this one in place,"

she said. George climbed on the lower one, then carefully crawled onto the second crate. He stood and stretched for the dog, but he was still a good six inches short.

"Come here, Jefferson," he called, but the dog didn't move.

Betsy watched him cajole and plead with Jefferson, but it did no good. She looked around for another crate, but the two they had stacked were fairly unstable even with her holding on. She didn't want to do it. She couldn't do it, but did she have a choice?

"Come down," she ordered her younger cousin, sighing impatiently. "I'll try to get him."

George quickly hopped down and took his place on the bottom crate.

"Hold this one tight," Betsy said as she crawled onto the second crate. She gingerly pulled herself to her full standing height.

"Tell him to face this way," she said.

George commanded his dog, but Jefferson didn't budge. Betsy reached for him and pulled his back end off the crate so that he had to shift his weight or fall. In an instant she had him in her arms.

"Jefferson," George shouted as he jumped up to take the dog. The crate he'd been steadying tipped, and Betsy grabbed the one above it to avoid taking a tumble. She felt Jefferson slide in her grasp, and she held him as tightly as she could with one arm.

"Sit down!" she shouted.

George plopped back down and steadied the second crate until Betsy had climbed down, then he popped back up and took the frightened dog in his arms.

"Jefferson," he cooed and stroked his dog on the forehead. "Don't run away like that again. You should have stayed with Betsy."

"Richard's violin!" Betsy cried. In her haste to chase Jefferson, she'd left it next to Silverstreak's hitching post. She dashed back down the street toward the horse and sighed with relief when she spotted the violin case and her lunch pail exactly where she'd left them.

George, with Jefferson's lead rope wrapped around his hand, loped up behind her. "You run fast for a girl," he said.

She nodded. Since she'd hemmed her skirt up to hide the holes Jefferson had created, she didn't have to hike up her skirt to run or even to walk. Not that she would forgive the dog for that.

"Father," George yelled as their parents made their way toward the hitching post. "Betsy saved Jefferson's life," he declared in a loud voice that stopped other pedestrians, who turned to hear the story.

All eyes focused on Betsy, and she blushed crimson as George explained about the crates and the other dog. George had a flair for the dramatic, and once again he had made her the center of attention even when she'd done him a good turn.

"You should see her run," George said. "She's so tall she has a long stride."

If possible, Betsy turned even redder.

"That's wonderful, Betsy," Mother said. "Let's gather our things and start for the inn."

Betsy gave her mother a grateful glance as the small group of travelers picked up their possessions and walked on.

"What about Silverstreak?" Betsy asked Father.

"I'll get him to a stable as soon as we get your mother settled."

Mother's skin was still pale, and her step was slow as they walked the block to the inn where they'd be spending two nights.

As soon as Mother and Betsy were in their room, Father left them to attend to traveling matters. He promised Betsy he'd show her around the city later that day.

It was after the evening meal before Betsy and Father knocked on the door to the Lankfords' room at the inn. Father had decided to take George along on their tour of Philadelphia, despite Betsy's protests. The last thing she wanted was to share her father with George! But Father had insisted George's parents would appreciate the silence George's absence would allow.

"Are all the details taken care of?" Uncle Paul asked when he answered the door.

"Yes. Our movings will be freighted on Monday and will arrive in Pittsburgh in a few weeks. Our stagecoach will leave promptly at six on Monday, so we must be at the stagecoach office shortly before then. Here are your tickets," Father said, handing them to Uncle Paul.

"Where are we going?" George asked, when Father had answered all of Uncle Paul's questions and the threesome were on the street outside the inn. Before Father could answer, George yelled, "A lamplighter. Do you think he'd let me light one?"

He didn't wait for an answer but flew down the street to the side of the man climbing the ladder beside the lamppost.

"What do you use for fuel?"

31

Betsy could easily hear George's excited question, but she had to strain to hear the lamplighter answer, "Whale oil."

"It sure smells. Could I light one?"

George followed the lamplighter to three posts before the lamplighter let him light one. The poor lamplighter must have figured that was the only way to get rid of the boy.

"Father, why don't you order George to stay with us?" Betsy asked. She normally wouldn't question Father's judgment, but George was back to his old tricks, being the center of attention.

"Oh, he's a boy and just naturally curious. If I thought he was annoying the lamplighter, I'd stop him. He learns a lot by asking questions. He's a smart boy."

Betsy stopped and looked at her father. Was he disappointed that his only child was a daughter? Did he want her to be more forthright and less shy? She couldn't help her personality, could she? She would never speak to a stranger the way George had just done.

"Did you see me?" George asked when he returned to Betsy's side.

"Yes," was her only reply.

Father showed them the state house where the Constitution had been signed. He pointed out the University of Pennsylvania, too.

"The medical school here is excellent. I visited the Pennsylvania Hospital briefly today and talked to several doctors about new procedures. Have you thought about becoming a doctor, George?"

So Father did want a son! He wanted someone to follow his lead and become a doctor. Betsy's posture slumped, and she looked down at the street as they walked along.

"I want to make things," George said. "Maybe ships like my father makes. Or maybe new things that haven't even been invented yet."

"There's a whole new world out there," Father said, "and we're going to be a part of it."

Betsy wanted to be part of it, too, but she felt that Father was talking only to George, a boy, a curious boy. She listened inattentively during the rest of their walk and was glad when they returned to the inn for the night.

At sunrise the next morning, the Millers and the Lankfords stood under the willows near the Navy Yard with hundreds of other worshipers for the Reverend William Staughton's service. The pastor was fiery in his delivery of the sermon. He shouted about human failings. He thundered about God's love.

When he read a verse from Isaiah about God's treatment of Israel, he caught Betsy's attention. "When thou passest through the waters, I will be with thee; and through the rivers, they shall not overflow thee. . ." Betsy knew he wasn't talking about their journey, but she took heart that God would be with them as they traveled. She dwelled on that while the pastor yelled about confessing. He roared about salvation. And he tore the air with his loud hallelujahs.

"He knows how to rile up a body," George said. He and Betsy followed behind their parents as they walked back to the inn.

"Yes, he's a powerful speaker," Betsy said. She much preferred the preacher at home who spoke more softly, but she had to agree that Pastor Staughton had reached a lot of people with his booming voice.

That was the biggest church service she had ever attended. No wonder it had been outside. A building couldn't hold that many people. And everyone had been quiet, so the preacher could be heard. Only the noise of the river had disturbed his words.

Betsy looked toward the Delaware River. Maybe Mother would let her go to the wharf this afternoon for a last look at the water that flowed to the sea, one of God's greatest creations. She shuddered at the thought that she might never see the ocean again.

CHAPTER FOUR
The Stinky Cheese

At daybreak the Millers and the Lankfords stood at the stage-coach office, loading their belongings onto the top of the stage. Betsy didn't trust the driver to safely anchor Richard's precious violin, so she stood in the doorway of the cab and leaned over the top.

"Move, George," she said. He had climbed all over the stage to inspect it and now sat on top in her way. He shifted a little and Betsy secured the violin between bags.

"Take your valise," Paul Lankford instructed his son.

"Here's another bag. Can you push it over there?"

Betsy ducked inside the cab. The interior of the stage allowed room only for passengers, and this time the six of them would be traveling alone. Even though George was small, there wasn't room for another person.

Betsy was appalled that Jefferson was allowed inside the coach with them. She sat beside the door and hoped George and his dog would be against the other door on the other side. That would be as far away from him as she could get in the cramped interior.

Within a few minutes everything was loaded. The driver came out of the stagecoach office with a satchel. "U.S. Mail" was printed on its side.

"He's putting it in the front boot, under the driver's box," George informed her. He had his foot on the passenger step, and of course he sat down on the bench seat directly opposite Betsy.

"Heyah," the driver yelled at the two teams of horses, and they were off.

George kept up a constant stream of chatter, pointing out landmarks they'd already seen as they rode across the uneven streets. Betsy figured he'd give a tree-by-tree description as they traveled the three hundred miles to Pittsburgh, but she watched the landscape move by, too.

Soon they approached the bridge over the Schuylkill River and awaited their turn to cross. The clomping of the horses' hooves echoed as they crossed the first long wooden expanse. Betsy had never been on a bridge this tall before, and she strained to see over the edge into the water below. George was hanging out the window.

"Look how high we are," he said. "How would you make a bridge like this?"

"In sections," his father answered. He poked his head out the other side of the stage. "Each arch is supported by stone piers. It's like a wharf, but it goes across the river instead of into the bay. It has to be tall enough to allow sailing vessels to pass underneath."

They were headed downhill now as they had crested the first arch, and Betsy braced herself against the window. Their descent was quick, but going up the steep second arch was a long process. By the time they had descended the final arch, Betsy was ready for level ground. As they rounded a curve and she could look back at the three arches, she saw another stagecoach on the bridge. Its passengers were walking across the bridge so the horses would have an easier pull.

Traveling was tiring, Betsy discovered. They jolted along at a fairly good clip on the turnpike, and every ten miles they stopped and paid a toll. Every time they stopped, George jumped out and let Jefferson run around. Betsy checked on Silverstreak, who was tied to the back of the stagecoach.

By dusk, Betsy was ready to scream. Jefferson had climbed all over her and everyone else. Good thing he was a little dog, but that didn't change her opinion of him licking her shoes and barking when they passed any wildlife or livestock. She tried to take a nap, but every time she'd nod off, they'd hit a bump and her head would hit the back of the cab.

She ached all over when they stopped for the night at an inn beside a toll booth. There weren't enough beds, since other travelers had stopped before them, so she claimed the floor with the quilts she'd used for cover in the cold coach.

Next to her was Richard's violin and her lunch pail. Even with the lid on, the pail leaked whiffs of the putrid cheese. She was tired of carrying the pail, and she was ready to get on with the plan of keeping George from being the center of attention. Certainly today he had monopolized the conversation.

"We're going fast," he'd said, after their third stop to pay the toll. "It won't take us long to get there."

"Eight days," Father had told him.

"It won't take us eight days at this speed," George had said.

"This is the easy part," Father said. "We're on level ground. We have to cross the mountains."

"It may take us a while going up, but coming down should be real fast," George had reasoned. "We could make it in seven days."

"You're using good logic," Father had said. "It does take longer to go up than come down, but the mountains will take longer than if we were on level ground, like now."

How could Father talk to George like that without yelling, "It'll take eight days! Now be quiet."

As she lay on the pallet on the floor of the inn, Betsy thought of how she could use the cheese. She doubted she could get it into George's valise without someone seeing her. However, she might be able to smear the cheese on the handles. When they loaded their belongings that morning, Uncle Paul had picked up the valise by the bottom and held it up so that his son could grab the handles. If they followed that pattern tomorrow, George would get smelly cheese all over his hands. Knowing George, he'd rub his hands on his clothes and make them smelly, too. Then he'd have to ride up with the driver in the cold wind. And he not only wouldn't be the center of attention, the silence in the cab without his chatter would give the others a welcome rest.

Betsy set the lunch pail near the fire so the cheese would soften in the night and fell asleep thinking that Mary would be pleased with her. When they got to Pittsburgh, Betsy would write to her friend and tell her how well the cheese worked.

Early the next morning, as soon as they had breakfasted, Betsy slipped outside with her gear. The temperature was nicer, more like spring, but the air still held a bit of winter's chill. She stowed the violin in the rear boot and set her lunch pail on the side of the stage that couldn't be seen from the inn. She stuffed the quilts and her cloak in the cab. She'd smear the cheese before she put on the bulky cloak, so it wouldn't get in her way and she wouldn't soil it. The driver was hitching the horses, but he paid no attention to her. Where were the others? She stepped back into the inn.

"George, are you ready?" She couldn't see him in the dining room.

"He's out back getting Jefferson," her mother answered. "Could you carry this please? Your father is fetching Silverstreak, and I think we'd better hurry before our driver gets impatient."

Betsy picked up the bag. "I can carry another one. Is George's valise ready?"

"Why, thank you, dear," Aunt Eleanor said. "It's right here." She pointed to it and then gathered her own belongings.

Betsy fairly skipped outside. This was better than the plan, but she didn't have much time. She heaved her mother's bag onto the luggage rack, then disappeared behind the stage to do her duty on George's valise.

The smell of the cheese nearly gagged her. It had gotten stronger in the tightly closed pail. She quickly opened the package, careful to keep her hands on the packaging and not touch the moldy cheese. She smeared the handles with the soft cheese, and for good measure spread some on the top, too. Then she quickly ran to the bushes on the far side of the road and tossed the cheese. Mother and Aunt Eleanor were on the small porch, and Father, Uncle Paul, and George were coming around the side of the inn.

"Load them up," the driver called. Betsy giggled. She'd actually done it without being seen. She sauntered toward the group and petted Silverstreak while Father tied the horse to the back of the coach. Another stagecoach was loading behind them, and the driver yelled "Load them up," again.

Betsy stood on the passenger step and started to climb into the cab, but Father stopped her. He'd come around to the side where George's valise sat on the ground.

"Find a place for this, Betsy," he said.

"But that's George's bag," she said. "Where's George?" She glanced inside the cab and saw George already in his normal seat, holding Jefferson.

"Hurry," Father said. He was holding the bag on the bottom and handing it up to her. He wrinkled his nose and glanced around as if looking for the source of the odor. What could she do? She froze.

"Betsy?"

She reached for the handle, trying to lift the bag with two fingers, but it was too heavy, and she had to take it from her father with a firm grip. She could feel the slimy cheese residue on her hand, but held her breath and shoved the bag on top of the coach. The valise teetered, so she wedged her foot against the wheel rim and hoisted herself up to stuff the bag in place. At that moment the impatient horses shifted, causing the wheel to turn slightly. Betsy lost her foothold and pitched headlong onto George's bag.

She gagged and pushed herself off the luggage rack. The stuff was in her hair, on her face, on her hands. She screamed, and Father reached for her.

"Don't touch me," she shrieked and jumped off the stage. She whirled around and saw the others staring at her from inside the cab. She'd made herself the center of attention. *Stop,* she told herself. *Calm down.* She had to get the cheese off.

Father leaned toward her, then backed away. "Betsy, what's that smell?"

"Limburger cheese," she mumbled and darted to the well at the side of the inn. She lowered the bucket and pulled it up, spilling cold water on her dress.

"Betsy, what have you done?" Mother had climbed out of the stage and stood beside her. "What is this in your hair?"

"Limburger cheese," Betsy said again, this time more plainly. She plunged her hands into the water and splashed some on her face, scrubbing at the cheese.

"You can't wash your hair now and travel all day with wet hair. You'd catch your death of cold," Mother said. "Where did you get this cheese?"

"On George's bag," Betsy said.

"George Lankford," Mother called toward the stage. "Get out here this minute."

"No, Mother. He didn't put it there. I did," Betsy said in

a small voice.

"Load them up," the stage driver yelled.

"We've got to go," Mother said. "We'll straighten this out on the way."

They walked back to the stage, and Mother climbed inside. Jefferson barked and jumped out of George's arms and onto the narrow floor when Betsy sat down by the window.

"You stink," George said.

She ignored him.

Jefferson growled, then he howled, and he backed away from Betsy.

The stage lurched and pulled away from the inn, and the chaos inside the coach grew louder.

"Make Jefferson stop," Betsy commanded.

"He can't help it. You smell bad," George said.

Betsy glanced at the others. George's parents looked bemused. Father's nose was wrinkled, and his eyes were sharp on her. She couldn't bring herself to look at Mother.

They were disappointed in her behavior, and they had a right to be.

"It was a harmless prank," Mother said in a loud voice to be heard over Jefferson's whining. "Where did you get the cheese?"

"I brought it from Boston." Betsy could have placed the blame on Mary, but that wasn't honest. Mary may have given her the cheese, but she hadn't forced her to use it. Betsy was already in big trouble. To lie would have made it worse. That was one of God's commandments, and Mother said to break one was a sin.

"You put it on George's valise?" Aunt Eleanor asked.

"Yes."

"Why?" Father asked.

What could she say? That George teased her too much, and she couldn't stand it anymore? That she wanted to make him pay? That Father really wanted a son and he was stuck with her? A too-tall gangly girl.

Jefferson let loose with a long howl and some short yaps, saving Betsy from answering.

"This can't continue," Mother said. "Thomas, would you ask the driver to stop? Betsy had better sit outside until she airs out."

"But, Mother," Betsy began, then stopped. She deserved this. She deserved to be punished. And she couldn't stand the yelping of Jefferson anymore. At least sitting outside she'd be away from George and his dog.

Father hailed the driver, who pulled up on the reins. The gruff fellow didn't look any too happy to have a smelly passenger sitting beside him on the driver's box, but he scooted over to make room for Betsy.

The March wind whipped against her, and she shivered into the quilt that she wrapped tightly around her, keeping her hands deep in the folds. She wished she could put on her hat, but with the cheese smell still in her hair, the hat would be ruined.

When they stopped to pay the first toll, George jumped out of the stage with Jefferson.

"How's the weather up there?" he called, but Betsy ignored him. She wallowed in her misery, and although her conscience argued with her, she vowed to find another way to teach George a lesson.

CHAPTER FIVE
The Embarrassing Horse Ride

At the end of the second day of travel, under the watchful eye of her mother, Betsy scrubbed the cheese off George's valise and apologized for playing what the family was calling her harmless prank. She took a bath, washed her hair, washed her too-short traveling dress, and hung it in front of the inn's fireplace to dry.

The point of her whole ordeal with George was to make him as miserable as he'd made her by embarrassing her. And that plan was to get him isolated, to not let him be the center of attention that he seemed to thrive on. All she'd managed to do so far was embarrass herself. She sat in front of the fire and finger-combed her hair until the curly brown locks were dry.

"I'm sorry," she'd heard her mother say to Aunt Eleanor. "That action was so out of character for our shy Betsy. I don't know what got into her, but I'll talk to her."

And her mother did talk to her. It wasn't a discussion; it was a lecture about how unladylike her conduct had been. About how it wasn't the Christian thing to do to play pranks on George. About how we must all get along on this trip. About right and wrong.

She knew all that. And she knew she had been wrong. The next time she planned how to get George, it would not involve other people.

How did George so effortlessly hurt her feelings? Did he plan those things out? Or was it a natural part of his personality to embarrass her? She would teach him to think more about other people's feelings. How exactly to do that escaped her for the moment, but she gave it a lot of thought as the journey continued.

The days of riding in the stage fell into a pattern. Part of the time they were walking, letting the horses pull the stage up the steep mountains without the added weight of passengers.

"We may as well have walked to Pittsburgh," George complained.

"At least we're not carrying our bags," Betsy had pointed out to him, one of the few times she directed a sentence his way. Mostly she stayed to herself, out of George's way.

She missed Boston. She missed Mary. What would she

be doing now? Did she go down to the harbor to look for Richard?

On Sunday, the group didn't observe a day of rest.

"I believe the Lord will understand that we must travel," Mother told Betsy. "Although He also must know how weary we are from the trip."

Father led an early worship service before they climbed back into the stage, and Betsy played a hymn on the violin. She found solace in her music, and she prayed that she would find a happy life in Cincinnati. She desperately needed a new friend.

"Today's the eighth day," George announced on Monday. "We'll get to Pittsburgh today, won't we?"

"We should," Father answered. He was still as patient as ever with George, to Betsy's dismay. "I suspect it will be early evening when we arrive."

George talked a blue streak the entire day. He asked about Pittsburgh, about building the flatboat, about where they would stay, about when they would leave for Cincinnati.

But it was Betsy who spotted Pittsburgh first. The telltale sign was the haze of smoke that hung over the horizon.

"They have factories," Father said. "Lots of them, and they burn coal. That's what makes all that haze."

They were still a few hours from settling in for the night. They had to wait for their turn on the ferry that would take them into Pittsburgh where they'd stay in yet another inn.

All along the riverbank were little wooden huts. Children scampered around, shouting as they played tag. Their voices carried to the ferry dock and combined with the sound of hammering from across the river. It was quite a noisy din.

Betsy's senses were reeling from the smoke and the noise. Pittsburgh wasn't the country town she had thought it would be. It reminded her of the manufacturing part of Boston. Would Cincinnati be like this, too?

Once they were settled at an inn for the night, Betsy fell into a deep sleep and awakened again to the clattering of hammers.

"What are they building?" she asked Mother at breakfast. Both families were grouped around the large table at the inn.

"Boats, of course, but there are a lot of foundries for iron-works, too. We'll explore today while your father and Uncle Paul make inquiries about the boat."

"Can I go to the stable and see Silverstreak?" This time Betsy turned to her father.

"That would be very helpful," he said and told her the name of the stable and gave her directions. "She could use a good grooming and some exercise, but that will have to wait. Your uncle Paul and I want to see if there are some adequately built flatboats before we make lumber purchases to build our own."

"Can I go with you?" George asked.

"It would be best if you stayed with the women today," his father replied. "Once we start building, you'll be part of the crew."

"If we build," Father said, "it will take awhile, and we won't be able to make the trip with the others when the thaw comes. The innkeeper said at the first sign of the spring floods, the river is crowded with boats."

"But we aren't going as far as the Louisville Falls. We're stopping at Cincinnati, so we don't need the high water,"

Uncle Paul said.

The two men left, still discussing whether to buy a boat or build it.

"Can we go down by the river?" George asked.

"Perhaps you and Betsy can after we walk around this area," his mother said. "I don't want you down there alone."

Wonderful, Betsy thought. She had to watch out for George again.

Betsy coughed when they walked outside the inn. The haze was the same as yesterday. Women on the street wore black with a little white lace peeking out of their bonnets and collars. She imagined they had to change the white lace quite often. Everything seemed various shades of gray.

The foursome walked the area around the inn, George in the lead with a long rope tied around Jefferson's neck and Betsy and the women following behind. They paused to glance inside the brick mercantile stores that lined the streets.

"We should make a list of supplies we'll need," Mother said to Aunt Eleanor. "There are plenty of mercantiles here with everything we'll need in Cincinnati."

"I wish we knew what could be purchased there and what we must take with us," Eleanor said. "Perhaps the men will know more when they return."

They walked down one side of the street for several blocks and up the other side of the street, then returned to the inn.

"You may go to the stable now, Betsy. Do you remember the way?" Mother asked. Betsy nodded, for she had noted the stable's location on their walk.

George piped up, "Can I go with her and then to the river?"

"That will be fine, but be back before noon," Aunt Eleanor said. No one had asked Betsy if it was all right for George and Jefferson to tag along. She sighed. Was there no escaping this boy and his dog?

He dashed ahead of her, staying in sight, so she didn't have to walk with him. When he reached the corner where they were to turn to get to the stable, he waited.

"Hurry up, Betsy."

On purpose she slowed her step. It was a small victory, but this was her errand, and she wouldn't be bullied about by George. Once she made the corner, George again ran along ahead of her, stopping now and then to look at stores or businesses.

She didn't know what his hurry was. When he reached the Blackburn stable, he didn't go inside in search of the horse, but stayed outside.

"Coming in?" Betsy asked as she swept regally by him.

"No, Jefferson and I'll wait, but don't take long. I want to go down by the river."

Betsy ducked inside the dimness of the stable and found the mare with no difficulty, even though she was in the last stall on the left. A stableboy was brushing a horse in a stall she passed, but she walked like she knew what she was doing, and he didn't bother her. She gave Silverstreak a good grooming, knowing that would please Father, and leaned her head against her only friend. She wished she could take the mare out for a ride. And why not? Silverstreak needed the exercise, and Father would be grateful that she'd done it.

She'd have to talk to the stableboy, and that wasn't something she wanted to do. Maybe she could get George to do it.

She strode purposely back outside.

"What kept you so long?" George asked.

"We're going to take Silverstreak out for a ride. Tell the stableboy what we're doing," she ordered.

"I'm not riding that horse," George said. "Come on. Let's go down to the river."

"We can ride Silverstreak and get there a lot faster."

"I'm not riding that horse," George repeated.

"Are you afraid of her?" Betsy asked. Surely not. But now that she thought about it, he'd given the horse a wide berth the entire trip on the boat and in the mornings and evenings when she and Father had tied Silverstreak behind the stage.

"I'm not afraid of anything," George said. "I want to walk, so we can look in the storefronts and see everything. Besides Jefferson can't ride."

"Oh," Betsy said. "Well, come talk to the stable boy."

"No, you want to ride, you talk to him."

Betsy took a deep breath. She couldn't talk to a complete stranger, could she? She heard Silverstreak's neigh from inside the stable, and her desire to exercise the horse and make Father think she was useful was stronger than her fear.

Please, God, give me courage, she silently prayed as she pivoted and marched back into the stable. She explained to the boy, who was probably only a year or so older than she.

"I can see the horse knows you," he said and helped her saddle the horse with a saddle that rested over a rail. It wasn't a side saddle like she was used to, but that was okay. She'd ridden on Father's saddle once and had found it gave her better control of the horse.

The next time she exited the stable, it was atop the mare.

"Ready, George?" She didn't mind being high above him this time. From her perch on the mare, she could see him scurrying ahead, pulling Jefferson behind him.

He darted down Market Street for a block and then turned immediately onto Water Street. There was the Monongahela River.

Children played among the wooden shacks. Clotheslines sagging with laundry were strung between the shanties. Someone yelled, "Tomorrow's the day. It's thawing." Men scurried about, carrying crates to the flatboats that lined the banks. Boys threw rocks at the thin ice that hugged the shoreline.

All this activity caused Silverstreak to neigh and rear. Betsy held on and reined her in, but the boys and girls stopped their play and ran over to see the horse.

"Is it yours?" a bold boy asked.

Betsy didn't answer. George had sidestepped away from the horse, but now he drew a bit closer.

"It's her father's horse, but she gets to ride it sometimes," he said.

"Can I ride it?" the boy asked.

"Sure," George said. "Can't he, Betsy?"

The cold of the March day didn't bother Betsy anymore. She felt her cheeks flush. "George," she hissed in a low voice. "You know I can't let anyone else ride her without Father's permission."

He shrugged his shoulders as if saying that was her problem, not his. Like always he was trying to be the good guy, be liked by everyone, be the center of attention.

"I have to get her back to the stable," she said. "George, come on."

"I'll stay here," he said and squinted at the sun that struggled to burn a hole through the hazy air. "It's not noon yet."

"Let us ride the horse," the boy spoke up again.

Betsy didn't answer.

"Ah, she's the only one with legs long enough to reach the stirrups," George said. "Let's do something else."

Betsy glanced down to see that a length of leg was showing below her dress on both sides of the man's saddle.

Mortified, she pulled the reins to the left and turned Silverstreak. She dug her heels into the horse's sides, and the mare cantered away from the group of children.

CHAPTER SIX
A Muddy Mess

Betsy stood at the edge of the group of crude dwellings and watched George in action. She'd groomed Silverstreak after she'd returned the mare to the stable, then trudged to the river. She wished Aunt Eleanor hadn't asked her to keep an eye on George. If Aunt Eleanor hadn't actually said the words, Betsy would have left him and returned alone to the inn.

George fit right in with the other boys. He didn't tower

over them, like she did. He had their attention, too, like always.

"Toss it in here, Johnny," he directed one of the boys. So he already knew them by name.

Johnny dropped a wooden contraption, which Betsy guessed was supposed to be a miniature flatboat, into the river. The boys ran along the side, tracking its progress.

"Look at it go now," George shouted. "The current's got it."

"It's gone," Johnny called. "Long gone."

A bulky-looking man strode quickly to the boys. "Did you use my good lumber for that toy? And my nails?"

"We thought we could catch it," Johnny explained. "George thought it up."

"Get back to the hut," the man ordered. "You boys find something else to do."

The boys dispersed in different directions. George glanced around, then headed for Betsy.

"Hey, it's the girl who wouldn't let us ride the horse," a boy said in a loud voice.

"We'd better get back," George said, as if he hadn't done anything wrong.

Betsy stared at him, then walked away from the river without saying a word.

As soon as they'd eaten the noon meal, Betsy asked her mother for paper and a quill pen.

"I thought you'd be wanting to write," Mother said as she rummaged in the trunk for the items. "I'll post a letter to your uncle Charles and aunt Martha and tell them of our progress. Perhaps they've heard from Richard by now."

Betsy sat at the small table in their room and wrote:

Dear Mary,
How I miss you. Have you gone to the wharf to look for Richard? I miss him, too. And I miss the ocean.
George is worse than ever. He talks to every stranger we see, desperate to get attention, even from those he doesn't know. The Limburger cheese got all over me instead of George. It was awful. I had to ride with the driver of the stage instead of out of the wind inside the cab.
Today George made fun of me in front of some strange children by the river here in Pittsburgh. I was on Silverstreak and my legs were showing below my dress. That is the worst thing he's done.
I have to think of ways to get him back. I'm out of room on this sheet, but I'll write again when we get to Cincinnati.

All my love,
Betsy

"I'm finished, Mother," Betsy said.

Her mother took the page and folded it twice and twice again, then wet a wafer and glued the edge. "Write Mary's name and Boston on here. As soon as I write my letter, we'll find the post office. I want to send these postpaid. We don't want to force a hardship on Mary when she picks up the mail."

Betsy nodded. If the embargo had affected Mary's family

as she'd hinted, she might not have an extra twenty-five cents to pay for the letter. She wrote the address and then let her mother have the table as a writing surface. Betsy sat on the bed and read from her book of poetry until her mother was finished. Mother asked the innkeeper about the post office, then the two set out the few blocks to post their letters.

"Betsy, is something wrong?" Mother asked as they walked along. "You're even quieter than ever. Is it George? You didn't say a word to him over our meal."

"George delights in embarrassing me. He made fun of me when we were at the river." Betsy told her mother about the incident.

"I don't think George intends you any harm. He's high-spirited, and he doesn't think before he says things."

"He's mean, and I want to embarrass him."

"Hmm. So that's why you put the Limburger cheese on his valise. Betsy, do you think God wants you to get even with George?"

Betsy hesitated, then said slowly, "I think He wants George to learn to respect other people."

"Yes, I believe that's true. But do you think it's up to you to teach George? Wouldn't that be his parents' job?"

"I don't see them doing anything about it. George doesn't say bad things when they're around. Except 'How's the weather up there?' "

Mother smiled. "I'm sure that can get irritating. We have the opposite problems. When I was your age, I was the shortest person in my class in school. The other girls and boys used me as a measuring stick. Each time someone passed my height, he bragged about it to the others. It wasn't long until the only ones who were shorter than me were those several years younger."

They had arrived at the post office, and Mother talked with the postmaster and paid for the letters to be sent to Boston. On their walk back to the inn, Betsy returned the conversation to her mother's problem.

"Did you ever want to get even with those children who made fun of you?"

"At first I did. But through the years I learned to accept myself as I was. And my mother talked to me about our Lord wanting us to turn the other cheek. He wants us to forgive those who trespass against us, rather than get even with them."

"But, Mother, that's easy for you because you're so beautiful. Others want to be like you. Nobody wants to be like me." Betsy blinked back tears.

"That's not true, dear. You're so pretty with those blue eyes. When you're excited about something, they sparkle so. And your hair—all those curls and that rich brown color. Aunt Eleanor's commented on how lucky you are to have such curly hair. Your height should be an asset. You should stand tall and regally. You're growing into a real beauty, Betsy."

"You're my mother. Of course, you would think so," Betsy said, but she felt better.

"Just wait. In a few years you'll have lines of suitors waiting to have you notice them. And you must be kind to each one of them, just like you must be kind to George now. He's impetuous and doesn't always think before he blurts out something. Forgive him and forget it."

Betsy mulled over her mother's words that afternoon as she walked to the shops again with the women. At least

George had convinced his mother to let him go to the river on his own. Later that evening the Lankfords joined the Millers in their room to discuss the next phase of the journey.

"Then we're going to build?" George asked.

"Yes," George's father said with a grin. "We've ordered lumber delivered to a site where we can work on it. The flatboats we saw aren't sturdy enough, and the lumber isn't the quality we want in our houses."

Betsy thought that was an established fact from the way Father and Uncle Paul had talked that morning. Father always wanted to check every option, but Uncle Paul had pushed for building the flatboat since before they had left Boston.

"I saw lots of flatboats at the river today," George said. "They said the wind shifted, and the thaw is here. Can I help build our boat?"

"Of course," Uncle Paul said. "We're going to need all the help we can get, so we can build it quickly. We can use your help, too, Betsy."

Everyone turned to look at her, and she tried to shrink further into the bed where she was sitting. She didn't know what she could do to help, and she sure didn't want to be around George day after day. Even though she was going to try to forgive and forget like Mother had suggested, staying away from George would be the easiest way to do that. On the other hand, this might be her chance to show Father that she was as good as a boy. He'd seemed pleased about her exercising Silverstreak and had said that working with her horse could be her daily chore.

"Eleanor and I have started a list of supplies we'd like to

take with us," Mother said. "We'll start shopping tomorrow. When will our movings arrive, Thomas?"

"Not for another couple weeks," Father said. "Freight travels slowly. Even though the teams of oxen are strong, pulling loads up those mountains will take some time. If we're going to get an early start on the flatboat tomorrow, we'd better turn in."

George's family left for their own room, and after everyone got ready for bed and Father said the nightly prayer, he blew out the lantern. Betsy lay on her pallet on the floor and stared through the darkness toward the ceiling. What was she doing in Pittsburgh, Pennsylvania? What sort of life waited for her in Cincinnati? Would the air be foul like here? Would there be a lot of children like the ones who lived in the shacks by the river? Those were travelers, waiting for the thaw, so they would be moving on. But would there be a lot of children in her new town? Would there be someone like Mary? And someday would there be lines of suitors wanting to meet her like Mother said?

The next morning at breakfast, the inn vibrated with activity. Travelers, who had lived at the inn instead of in the huts by the river, bustled about preparing to leave.

"The thaw's here. We're shoving off," one man said. "The river rose ten feet last night."

"Can I go watch?" George asked. "Can I?"

"I suppose," his mother answered. "If Betsy will go with you. There's too much activity for you to go alone today."

"She'll go. Won't you, Betsy?" George said. Betsy glanced at her mother, who had raised her eyebrows as if to tell her this was her chance to forgive and forget.

"All right," she said and nodded.

"Stay out of the way of the travelers," Mother said.

George raced outside to get Jefferson, and Betsy followed more slowly. She had changed from her too-short traveling dress. She wanted to present as respectable as possible a picture of herself.

"Come on," George shouted. "We'll miss them leaving."

Highly unlikely, Betsy thought, and was stunned when they arrived at the river to find half the flatboats already gone. Unlike the waiting attitude of yesterday, today the air was filled with excitement. People on board the boats called good-byes to those still on shore, and polemen called orders from one side of the boats to the other. Betsy lifted her long skirt and stepped gingerly to avoid soft ground and mud holes created by earlier melting snows.

"Stay back here," she told George as she watched men trying to coax livestock on board. Horses neighed and cows mooed as men lead them onto flatboats. Jefferson barked. Some boys were chasing chickens and putting them in a coop when they caught them.

"Hold Jefferson," George said and thrust the dog's rope into Betsy's hand. George jumped in the fray and chased the chickens toward the boys, although he didn't make any move to catch any of the hens.

"Fresh eggs for the journey," a girl said, who opened and shut the coop's door as the boys stuffed the fowl inside.

"Maybe fried chicken would be better," George said.

Jefferson yelped and ran around and around Betsy, twisting the lead rope.

"Stop that," she ordered, and took a few steps forward, trying to get the dog under control. He was headed straight for a muddy area. Too late. The dog circled her again and the rope bound her legs together. She tottered, was unable to catch her balance, and plopped backward on the muddy ground.

Jefferson barked and jumped on her with his muddy paws, and Betsy stuck her hands in the soft ground to lever herself up. It was no use. She'd only succeeded in getting her hands covered with muck. She pushed the dog away, but he barked and howled and jumped back on her, trying to free himself from the tangled rope that still bound Betsy.

"What are you doing?" she heard George shout.

She glanced up and saw George and the other boys running toward her.

"It's all right, Jefferson. I'll free you," George cooed to his dog.

"Jefferson! What about me?" Betsy exclaimed. The boys were laughing now, and she felt that familiar heated flush creep up her cheeks. Forgive and forget. That's what her mother had said. But her mother didn't spend time around George and his smelly dog. Her mother wasn't the one who now sat in a mud hole with her dress wet and filthy and at least seven boys laughing at her.

"Johnny, come load," a voice called, and the boys dispersed, leaving George wrestling with the rope.

"Lift your feet," he said, and Betsy struggled to get the rope untangled.

Finally it was unwound from her legs, and George held the lead rope in his hands. Jefferson no longer danced around and yelped. He sat quietly beside his master.

Betsy pushed herself to her feet.

"We are going back," she said. "Come, now."

"But I'm helping them load and everything," George said.

"I said now and I mean it." With all the aplomb she had, a muddy Betsy walked tall and regally toward the street that lined the river. George and his dog followed.

CHAPTER SEVEN
Building the Flatboat

By late afternoon, Betsy returned to the river's edge with Mother and Aunt Eleanor and George. Betsy wasn't about to take George down there by herself, and Mother had agreed with her after she'd helped Betsy clean up and wash out her dress. So they all set out for a walk. Jefferson was tied to a post behind the inn.

The riverfront village was deserted. Flatboats that had lined the river had cast off from the landings and were already on their way to points west. Although the din of hammering and sawing from factories still reached Betsy's ears, they were sounds she was becoming used to. Now the silence of the riverfront was eerie. No children's shouts and laughter split the air. The bustle of the morning could have been in her imagination.

"We missed it," George said, as if it were Betsy's fault.

"There will be more travelers through here," Mother said. "I heard talk at the inn about this being a late start for the first leaving. It's usually in February, but this year winter stayed longer. We'll still have high water when we can start our journey again, with no chance of ice chunks to harm our boat."

"Who told you that?" George asked. "Maybe I can talk to him."

"For what reason?" Aunt Eleanor asked her son.

"To find out more about the travelers. Maybe more boys will live here for a while. Somebody to play with," he said with a sideways glance at Betsy.

He'd better look for someone else to play with, Betsy thought, because it sure wasn't going to be her.

"There won't be much time for play," Aunt Eleanor said to her son. "If the men get their lumber delivered today, they'll be ready to begin on the flatboat tomorrow. Your father drew up plans for it before we left Boston. He's anxious to get started, and he's counting on you for help."

"Oh, I want to help," George said. "I like building things."

The foursome walked six streets from the river to the public square, the Diamond.

"A lot of the wagons are gone," Aunt Eleanor said. "I

64

guess we should have walked farther around the square this morning."

"We got a lot of things on our list, and Saturday's another market day," Mother said. "I wonder how long we'll be in Pittsburgh."

She repeated the question that evening after dinner when the two families once again visited in the Millers' room.

"That depends," Father said, "on how many men we can find to help us build the boat. We've put the word out today that we'll be hiring and hope for men to come by the site tomorrow. The lumber is there and Paul has approved it."

"Not a knot in it," Uncle Paul said with pride. "You can't use knotted wood for a boat. Water pressure can push the knots out and sink the boat."

Early the next morning Betsy, George, Father, and Uncle Paul walked out to the building site. Betsy and George sat on lumber to weigh it down while the men sawed it to length.

"It'll be fourteen by fifty feet," Uncle Paul said. "Narrow enough to get through tight places and long enough to hold our movings."

"George, over here," Father called.

And that was the way most of the morning passed. Betsy held boards for Uncle Paul, and George held boards for Father. Betsy glanced over at Father, who was in a discussion with George. Of course, George could talk to a wall, so that was no surprise. But it rankled, just the same. Was Father thinking of George as the son he didn't have?

Betsy did exactly what Uncle Paul asked her to do, determined that she could do a boy's job as well as a boy and certainly better than George.

By late morning a few men had drifted to the site, asking about the job. And before noon, Father had hired three men and sent Betsy back to the inn. George was allowed to stay.

Betsy walked slowly back to their lodgings, wondering why Father preferred George to her. What had she done wrong?

She found her mother and Aunt Eleanor packing food from the inn to take to the men.

"They'll be too dirty to come in for the noon meal," Mother said. "So the innkeeper has allowed us to take food to them. We can use your help carrying."

"I can't go back," Betsy said. "Father doesn't want me there."

Mother set a pot of beans down on the table with a thump. "What did he say? What did you do? Why did he send you back here?"

"I don't know," Betsy said and held back a sob. She knew all right. He wanted George. He wanted a son.

"I'll talk to Thomas," Mother said thoughtfully. "This is unlike him."

Betsy carried a basket and followed the women the few blocks near the river where the men were laying out the framework of the boat.

"There are extra men here," Mother said in a low voice.

"Yes. Father hired them this morning."

"I see." The women left the food, and Mother said they'd come back for the pots and dishes a little later. She spoke a moment with Father, then walked back to join Betsy and Aunt Eleanor.

"A couple of the men are a little rough," Mother explained as they walked back to the inn. "Their language isn't something that Father wants you to hear."

"But he lets George hear it," Betsy said.

"I suppose since he's a boy, the men feel it won't offend him. Sometimes, Betsy, it's a mixed-up world. No one should speak in a manner that would offend another person. But that's not always the way it is. Your father wants to protect you from this."

So, she would not be allowed on the building site except to deliver food. George and her father would become even closer, and there was nothing she could do about it.

For the next week, Betsy shopped with the women and tightly packed their purchases in crates for the trip. She exercised Silverstreak each morning and afternoon and learned the city of Pittsburgh. She explored the ruins of old Fort Pitt and visited Grant's Hill on the eastern edge of the settlement. At the foot of the hill was Hogg's Pond, home to wild ducks and half-wild hogs. After the pigs caused Silverstreak to shy and almost unseat Betsy, she cut the pond from her exercise route.

And she secretly worked on a surprise for Father.

At noon she carried food to George and the men. George strutted around and practically crowed that he was allowed to participate in such an adult project as building a boat.

Most of the time, Mother and Aunt Eleanor accompanied Betsy, but on Wednesday of the second week, they had returned to the farmer's market and Betsy made the trip to the site by herself on horseback. Baskets of food were strapped across the horse, and after Betsy delivered the food, she waited for the men to eat so she could load it and return the utensils to the inn.

George had taken Jefferson out to the site and had him

tied to a post, but Betsy took no chances with the food. Once she had loaded the plates with fried chicken and bread, she put the pan of leftover chicken high on top of a pile of lumber, out of Jefferson's reach.

She retrieved it when the men asked for more chicken and served them.

"I want another piece," George said not one minute after she'd asked if he wanted more. She pretended not to hear him and asked Uncle Paul a question about the boat building. Out of the corner of her eye, she watched George get up and walk to the chicken. Good. He had to serve himself. He tried to reach the chicken, but it was over his head, so he jumped and grabbed for the handle of the pan. He succeeded in bringing the pan right down on his head. Since he was looking up, the handle hit him in the eye.

To Betsy, the accident seemed to take place in slow motion. She screamed and jumped up when she saw the heavy pot fall, but she couldn't reach George in time to prevent the injury.

Father examined the bump on George's head and the gash under his eye. Blood trickled from the wound. "Betsy, take George back to the inn. Wash his wound and put the white ointment on it that's in my bag. George, you get to take the rest of the day off to play. Your wound isn't serious, but you may develop a headache from that bump. Betsy will stay with you."

"I'll load up the pots and dishes, and we can walk beside Silverstreak," Betsy said.

Once she got him in the Millers' room at the inn, she obeyed her father's instructions. George winced, but didn't cry when she bathed the wound with well water.

"You're going to have a black eye," Betsy said. "It's already starting to turn."

"A shiner? I'm going to have a shiner?" George seemed elated with the information that would have mortified Betsy. How could he enjoy the prospect of having people stare at him and wonder what had happened to his eye?

"Probably take it a week to disappear," Betsy said, drawing on her knowledge of her father's experience. Sometimes in Boston she'd accompanied him on calls, so she could watch the patient's children, her father had said, but mostly she watched what he did for the sick.

When the women returned laden with more purchases, they made a fuss over George. But he seemed restless once the women went to the Lankfords' room to pack the household goods in crates.

"Let's go down to the river to see if any other travelers have come," he suggested.

"No. Father wanted you to rest, so you should remain quiet."

"But what's there to do here?" His hand motion took in the tiny room. "What do you do all day?"

Betsy didn't want to tell her younger cousin, but she felt responsible for his accident and wanted to make up for it. "I've been studying the *Navigator*." She held up a copy of the traveler's guide to the western rivers. "It tells how to get down the Ohio."

"Father has a copy of that, but reading isn't really doing anything."

"I'll be right back," Betsy said and left her room to fetch

Uncle Paul's copy of the *Navigator*. When she returned, she opened it and handed it to George.

"Look at this page on shoving off at Pittsburgh," she said. "There's a large flat bar at the mouth of the Allegheny, nearly meeting the foot of the Monongahela." She read aloud, "'There is, however, a good passage between these two bars, in a direction a little above the Point or junction of the two rivers, towards O'Hara's glassworks. Before you get quite opposite the Point, incline to the left, and you will get into the chute, keeping the foot of the Monongahela bar on the left hand, and the head of that of the Allegheny on your right.'"

"Sounds hard," George said.

"But it's not. Look," she said and drew a folded copy of the Pittsburgh newspaper, the *Gazette,* from the trunk. "I'm drawing pictures of the river on this paper. Try to block out the words and focus on my lines. See, here's the river and the two sandbars. This X is the glassworks. You've seen it across the river. This arrow shows the route we need to take to avoid the sandbars."

George examined her drawing. "This is good," he said, and Betsy let out a breath she was unaware she'd been holding.

What was she doing? She certainly didn't need George's approval of the way she was passing time waiting for the boat to be finished.

George flipped to the next drawing. "How far have you gone down the river?"

"Not too far. I have about eight maps drawn. How much longer will it take to build the boat?"

"It's going fast with so many workers," George said with pride in his voice. "We should caulk with oakum and pitch on Monday, but Father says he wants that to cure good before we turn the boat. While it's curing, we're going to start the walls of the cabin."

"But how long?" Betsy asked again. George was like Uncle Paul. He had details in his mind and couldn't answer a simple question with a simple answer. "Hard to say. It depends some on the weather. But I imagine in another two weeks of work we'll be ready to go."

Two weeks to work on her drawings. She could probably have them done by then.

CHAPTER EIGHT
Danger on the River

The boat turning took place two weeks after work had commenced on the flatboat. The large, awkward structure needed to be turned over so that the bottom could rest in the water. Extra hands were needed to wield the monstrous frame into the river. The men had rolled it to the water's edge on logs and then piled huge rocks on one side to weigh it down.

Betsy and George and the women helped some of the men

hold ropes to steady the boat as others lifted it with poles, setting and resetting them as the edge of the flatboat opposite the water lifted higher and higher. The weighted-down side was underwater, and within minutes of the pushing of the poles and pulling of ropes, the boat flipped over and settled on the Ohio River.

Cheers rang out from the workers, and Betsy joined in. Another phase of the building began as the workmen prepared to build up the sides and put a roof over the living quarters for the families.

"The hard part's done," George told Betsy as if he knew what was involved in building a flatboat.

"At least my part is done," Betsy said and dropped her rope. She and the women returned to the inn and the packing. Their movings had arrived by freight wagon and were being stored in one of the huts on the riverfront. Some of those crates needed repacking since they'd been damaged in the move.

"Good thing we got rid of so many things in Boston," Mother said. "How will we ever fit all of these crates on the boat?"

"We'll pile them high," Betsy said.

"Your father wants to buy glass here for our windows, but I don't know where we can put it. Perhaps he should purchase it and have it sent on the merchant ships. We can't take all the supplies it will take to build a house in Cincinnati."

The night after the boat turning, Father brought a man to the inn for dinner and introduced him as Marley.

"He's a bargeman who'll help us get down the Ohio," Father said. "Marley's made twenty trips down the Ohio. He knows every crooked turn of that river."

"And there are many," Marley said. He was a short, stocky man, but appeared to be all muscle, not fat.

"Betsy and I've made maps of the river," George said, and Betsy gasped. She'd let him work on the maps that one day when he'd gotten his black eye. It had healed now, but she felt like giving him another one. He was claiming responsibility for her work.

"Have you now?" Marley asked. "Can I see them?"

"Sure," George said. "Where are they, Betsy?" Almost as an aside he added, "Betsy did most of them."

With all eyes on her, Betsy excused herself and went to her room to get the maps. When she returned, George was explaining about the *Navigator* to Marley.

"I know the fellow who writes that guide, and he's thinking of putting maps in it someday. But it will take some time for him to draw them up and get them printed." Marley reached out and took the maps Betsy had drawn on the newsprint. The others crowded around his chair to look them over.

"Now this is some fine studying of the guide," Marley said. "You sure you haven't been on this river before?" He laughed a loud friendly laugh.

"This is fine work," Father said and looked directly at Betsy. "We'll rely on you and Marley to get us to Cincinnati without mishap."

"Oh, there'll be mishaps," Marley said. "Most folks think they're going on holiday when they set out. They think they can just sit and gab on the boat, but they learn soon enough that it's not that way. There's lots of work to be done to keep the boat in the current and not caught in an eddy or stranded on a sandbar."

Betsy had read enough to know exactly what he was talking about, but George looked a little puzzled. He probably thought he'd fish the whole time.

The men talked of the boat construction and when departure day would come. A new man had been hired to lay up the fireplace so they could cook on the trip. The brick would be used again for their house.

Although it was enlightening to hear these things, Betsy let her mind drift to the actual journey down the river. Now that she had studied the bends and curves and sandbars, she was anxious to begin the trip.

From under lowered lashes, she studied Marley. She had seen him in church the two times they had attended local services. He'd sung hymns in a deep bass voice. A loud voice. Much like his laughter. She supposed he was loud because of yelling orders on flatboats. His eyes twinkled when he caught her watching him, and she quickly looked down at her hands.

After he left, Father said that he had been searching for a Christian man to pilot them down the Ohio and was pleased that Marley had agreed.

"Be kind to him," he said to Betsy. "He's known some tragedy in his life." He didn't elaborate, and Betsy was left wondering what that tragedy was.

Another week passed. Betsy finished reading the *Navigator* as far as the Cincinnati port. Her mother had taken her to one of the two bookstores in Pittsburgh and let her pick out several books to add to her limited collection, calling them part of her education. They had intended to continue sums and writing and reading study, but her mapmaking study combined all three in a way that satisfied Mother. And that was fine with Betsy. She figured her schooling would be ahead of whatever type of school was held in Cincinnati.

Betsy accompanied Father to a chemist and mineralogist who was trying to establish a manufacture of acids. The doctor had already found many native materials for making drugs, and Father purchased several medicines to take to Cincinnati and arranged for further orders.

The day before leaving arrived, and the women helped the men load the boat. They evenly stacked crates and trunks in certain positions to guarantee a balanced boat.

"Can't have one corner in the water," Marley said. "Put that one down here, young George."

"Hold this blanket," Mother instructed Betsy. They strung it on rope as a room divider under the roofed area, separating the sleeping areas from the cooking and living area.

By nightfall, the boat was loaded and only lacked perishables and Silverstreak. Early the next morning, the travelers loaded the horse and George's dog and climbed on board, and the next phase of the journey began.

"Cast off that line," Marley ordered, and Uncle Paul unlooped the cable on the dock and jumped on board.

Betsy sat on a crate near the front of the flatboat with her maps in hand. Father held a great long oar on one side of the boat, and Uncle Paul did the same on the other. Marley steered from atop the roof with a long sweep that acted as a rudder.

Although she didn't say a word, Betsy watched with great interest as Marley maneuvered the boat between the sandbars of the Allegheny and the Monongahela that she had read about and mapped out. They shot by Hamilton's Island in a chute that was narrow and rapid, and then they were truly in the Ohio River.

Within minutes they had left the smoky haze and the noise of manufacturing behind them. Betsy sighed. Marley may have said it wasn't a holiday, but it seemed like one to her. The April sunshine warmed her all over, and George and his dog were at the stern behind the enclosed space and as far from her as possible. They floated past farmland and brushy undergrowth so thick she couldn't see through it.

"Push off toward the left," Marley called to Uncle Paul. Betsy admired the way her father and Uncle Paul worked in tandem, as if they could predict the other's move with his sweep.

As they rounded a bend, they met with head winds. Betsy pulled her cloak around her against the chill. For the next hour they made slow progress against the wind. Once around another curve, the wind switched again, and they picked up speed.

"How far will we get today?" she asked Marley, who had traded places with Uncle Paul, and was now manning one of the long poles.

"Depends. Could make twenty or twenty-five miles. Where do you have us on the map, little lady?"

He always called her that. At first Betsy thought he was making fun of her, since she was taller than he, but she soon discovered that "little lady" was his title of respect.

"I have us past Hog Island and headed for Dead Man's Island."

"Right on target. See those willow branches in the middle of the river?" He pointed. "Look to the left."

"Oh, yes, I see them."

"That's all you'll be seeing of Dead Man's Island. The water's still too high to show the land. But we know it's there, so the good Lord willing, we won't be caught unawares." He turned toward Father. "Get ready to move her to the right." He shouted orders to Uncle Paul, who stood atop the roof with a tight grip on the sweep.

George came back around the little house with Jefferson on his heels.

"Did you say Dead Man's Island? How many men have been killed there?"

Trust George to want gory details, Betsy thought.

"Too many to count," Marley said. "In flood times there's not even a leaf to warn travelers about the trees underneath the water. Many a flatboat has been stove in and sunk in a minute's time. Now, bear hard to the right," he shouted to Uncle Paul.

Within a few minutes they had successfully passed the ripples above Dead Man's Island and swept to the right of it.

"I like the fast water," George said. He fashioned a chair out of a crate and stuck his fishing line in the river.

"Do you have any bait?" Betsy asked.

"No. But I'm going to dig for worms when we land for the night. Then we'll have fish for supper tomorrow."

Betsy doubted it. She hadn't known George to be much of a fisherman, even in Boston. He was too impatient to sit still for long.

At noon the women served a lunch of beans that had

cooked all morning over the fire in the little house. The fire kept the shelter warm, and from time to time Betsy disappeared inside to stand by the fireplace. She checked on Silverstreak, who was tied at the stern and who seemed to be taking the riverboat ride in stride.

The afternoon passed pleasantly enough with the same atmosphere of peace and tranquillity. The silence was only broken by the low murmuring of voices on the boat, birds chirping, and an occasional fish near the bank, jumping and splashing. They met three keelboats working their way up the river and called to each one. Betsy never tired of watching the landscape pass by. There were hills, long forest slopes, and meadows. Trees had budded green, and occasionally a redbud and white dogwood brightened the underforest.

"We're going to be looking for a place to tie up for the night," Marley told Betsy late that afternoon. "We'll be wanting daylight to get our cable secured to shore and not be landing on any sandbars in the process."

Was he asking for her opinion? Surely not, but he looked at her with raised eyebrows.

"See any place on your map that looks good?"

Betsy consulted her well-thumbed copy of the *Navigator*.

"The book says that if we land, we'll have considerable loss of time and some hazard," she said.

"But we'll all be needing sleep, and if we keep going, we'll have to keep a good lookout to stay in the current. Your father's plan is to tie up at night and move on at first light."

Betsy bent over her maps. "After we clear the next bend, there's a little cove."

"I was thinking the same thing," Marley said. In a louder

voice he announced to the others that they were planning to land.

Around the next curve, there appeared to be a fork in the river, but Betsy knew it was deceptive. A peninsula stuck out far enough that travelers couldn't see around it as they could see around most islands. The Navigator warned that it had fooled many travelers who thought it was a shortcut to straighten out the river.

"We can't go too far in the cove, or it'll be hard to get out tomorrow," Marley said. "But we want our cable to reach both shores. If my memory serves me right, there's a tie-up tree on the left. Look there."

So Marley had known all along that this was where they would stay the night, Betsy mused. But he had been nice enough to ask her advice because she had worked hard on her maps.

Uncle Paul rowed in the skiff to the shore and secured one cable from the left side of the flatboat. Then he rowed to the shore of the peninsula and secured a cable from the right side of the flatboat.

"Can I go on the land?" George asked, once the boat was secured for the night. "I need to dig for some worms."

"I'll take George and Betsy ashore," Marley said. "There's a creek where we can fill the water buckets with cleaner water than we can pull out of the Ohio."

Although she wasn't keen on being in the skiff with George, Betsy longed to stretch her legs and explore a bit.

Marley rowed them the short distance to shore and pulled the skiff up on the bank so Betsy could get out without getting wet.

"Creek's right down that way, little lady."

While Marley showed George where grubs would be hiding under some downed limbs, Betsy carried one water bucket and wandered through the underbrush toward the creek that emptied into the Ohio. She gingerly watched her step on the uneven forest floor.

She wasn't fifty feet away from the creek when from the corner of her eye she caught a movement. She lifted her gaze to stare straight into the eyes of an Indian!

CHAPTER NINE
The Graves

Betsy froze. The Indian, a boy about her age, stood beside his horse, which was drinking from the creek. He said something that she couldn't understand.

He said it again.

Betsy finally found her voice and screamed, "Marley!"

"Marley?" the Indian repeated.

Betsy twirled when she heard running footsteps behind her.

Marley burst through the undergrowth with George on his heels. Marley looked at Betsy, then at the Indian. He said something in a different language to the boy, and the boy responded and grinned.

"It's okay, Betsy. This is Running Fox. We're friends."

"You know this Indian?" George asked.

Marley took on a haunted look. His eyes narrowed and a frown line crossed his brow. He breathed out a sigh. "He's from a settlement not far from here. I know it well."

"Then he's friendly?" Betsy asked.

"Very friendly," Marley said. Again he spoke to the boy in his native language. The boy answered and motioned behind him.

"He's been looking for a stray," Marley said.

Betsy heard a distant mooing that seemed to come from upstream.

The Indian boy cocked his head as if he'd heard it, too, and immediately mounted his horse. He called something to Marley, and Marley held up a hand in farewell.

"How do you know him?" George asked as they filled their buckets with creek water.

Marley hesitated, then said, "At one time I lived with the Indians. Let's get back to the boat. We need to settle in before dark."

Whatever Marley knew about the Indian boy and the settlement, he didn't want to talk about, Betsy quickly decided as they made their way back through the undergrowth toward the boat.

George stopped to pick up a small bag, which Betsy figured held his worms and grubs for fishing. She moved to his other side as far from the bag as she could get.

They climbed back into the skiff, and Marley rowed them to the flatboat. The evening settled around them. Father offered a prayer of thanks for the safe start on their journey, and they ate with the light from the lantern making soft shadows on the boat.

After dinner Betsy played a few tunes on the violin until Jefferson howled in competition with her music. Then she put the instrument away and sat near the edge of the boat, listening to the night sounds of the river.

George plopped down beside her.

"Why do you think Marley lived with the Indians?" he asked.

Betsy had been wondering about the same question. "I don't know. Did your father tell you anything about him?"

She couldn't see his face in the darkness, but Betsy could see by the way he tilted his head that he was trying to remember.

"He said they'd looked a long time to find someone like Marley to take us down the river. Most of the bargemen are rough, noisy men. They brag and fight each other a lot." George sounded like that was something he'd have liked to have seen.

Betsy nodded. "I heard Father tell Mother that Marley was a good Christian man who would fit in with us. He told me that Marley had known tragedy, and I should be nice to him."

"You think his tragedy has something to do with the Indians?"

Betsy shrugged. "Maybe."

"How are we going to find out?" George asked.

"I suppose we have to wait for him to tell us. And we aren't going to pester him, George. We may never know."

"I wonder if my father knows."

Again Betsy had been thinking along those same lines, and she wasn't pleased that she and George had the same thoughts. Still, she would look for an opportunity to talk to Father tomorrow.

The April night was chilly, and Betsy settled near the fireplace in the enclosed area to sleep. The others crowded in, and she didn't have room to roll over.

The next morning at dawn, the men untied the cables and shoved off with their long sweeping oars. They pushed off the river bottom for as long as their oars would reach, then rowed into the main channel of the wide Ohio.

George immediately tossed out his fishing line. Betsy edged over to her father's side of the boat.

"We need to take Silverstreak off the boat tonight if possible and give her some exercise," Father said.

"How can we do that?" Betsy asked. "She can't get in the skiff."

Father laughed. "You're right. Only if there is a landing can we take her off. We'll have to watch for a ferry landing or a wharf. It may be a day or two. Would you check the *Navigator*?"

"Yes, Father. Oh, I've been wondering about Marley," she said as if it were an afterthought. "He's a very nice man. What exactly tragic happened to him? Did it have to do with the Indians?"

"Turn port side," Marley called from his position high atop the roof. "Sandbar."

Father turned his attention to his long sweep and pushed hard against the bottom of the river. The boat moved toward the left and glided into the stronger current.

Betsy thought she would have to repeat her question, but Father turned back to her just then.

"Marley confided in me, and I cannot break his confidence. If you get to know him well, he may tell you of his past tragedy. He's known sorrow, but he's overcome it with God's help. It's his story to tell, not mine."

How could she get to know Marley? It wasn't in her nature to jabber on like George did at times. It had taken her courage to ask Father about him, and she wasn't really shy around Father. She knew he loved her, even though she still felt he wished she were a boy, and knowing that he loved her gave her courage to talk to him when she couldn't talk to others.

In Pittsburgh, Father had told her to be kind to Marley. She could do that. He had charged forward to rescue her from the Indian, even though it turned out she didn't need saving. He had been open to her few questions about their trip, and he had asked her about her maps. They were developing a solid friendship. She would treat him as she wanted to be treated, just as the Golden Rule said.

With that decided, Betsy spent the rest of an uneventful day enjoying the spring sunshine and studying the maps to find a place to exercise Silverstreak.

"Can we get to Steubenville by dark?" she asked Marley when he took a shift on the starboard side where she sat studying the guidebook.

"We've been doing well today. We might make it. Need to go shopping?" he teased.

Betsy laughed. "No. I need to take Silverstreak for a ride."

"Hey, Jefferson needs to run, too," George piped up. Betsy was unaware he had moved over to her side of the boat.

"Just keep him away from Silverstreak," Betsy said.

"There's plenty of room for you two to keep a distance," Marley said, and Betsy studied him. Did he know about her feud with George? They'd been getting along better, but she hadn't forgotten how he'd embarrassed her when the Pittsburgh settlement travelers were pushing off.

"There's a new courthouse at Steubenville," Marley said. "And a new jail, if we need to lock one of you up."

"Are there a lot of criminals there?" George asked.

"No more than anywhere else, I reckon," Marley said.

"Are they Indians?" George asked, and from Marley's expression, Betsy figured George had asked one too many questions.

"No," Marley said. "You have something against Indians?"

"No. Just wondering," George said, and he went back to where he had left his fishing line dangling in the water.

They traveled longer that day, and by dusk they arrived at Steubenville and tied up for the night. Father and Betsy unloaded the mare, but it was Father who rode her through the streets and out into the country.

"You'd better stay with the women," Father had said, "since it's near dark."

Although Betsy was allowed to walk the length of the

main street with the others, she'd hoped for the freedom of a ride on the horse. The cramped quarters of the boat bothered her. She'd been used to the limitless feel of gazing at the ocean. The river, although wide, was bordered by forests and fields and hills. It was a closed-in feeling. How did people inland adapt to this? The sea called to her, and she wanted to answer.

The sea reminded her of Richard, and she wondered where he was on this April evening when the first star could now be seen. Was he fighting on a British ship or was he back in Boston? Maybe once they were settled in Cincinnati they would hear from his folks.

"Let's get back on board," Mother said. "We need to fry up those fish, and Father will be back soon."

Betsy couldn't believe George had caught enough fish for supper, but he had, and he wasn't letting her forget it, either.

After the meal, Betsy laid down early for the night. Two days on the river, and the time ahead stretched out in front of her endlessly. What waited for them at journey's end?

At daybreak, the men pushed off again, and by midafternoon, they tied up at Wheeling.

"Betsy, it's your turn to exercise Silverstreak," Father said. "We'll only stop for an hour at most, so take care to be back here soon."

Betsy glanced at the sun's position, then rode the horse down Wheeling's one street. Once they passed the last building, she let Silverstreak have her head and run wild. The wind whipped Betsy's hair, and she celebrated her freedom by laughing aloud. All too soon she gauged the sun had drifted a half hour toward the western horizon, so she turned the horse back toward town.

"Fried chicken tonight," Mother announced once they were back on the river. "What luck that we landed here on market day."

Betsy groomed Silverstreak, then took up her usual position, sitting on a crate and studying her maps.

"Where are we tying up for the night?" she asked Marley.

"Near Little Grave Creek."

"The mounds," Betsy said with awe. The *Navigator* had given a detailed account of the ancient big mound and the smaller ones near it. "Can we explore?"

"I reckon if your folks say you can," Marley answered.

"What mounds?" George asked from the other side of the boat.

That boy had to have hearing that would put a dog to shame.

"Nothing really," Betsy said. "Just some big hill." There was no reason George needed to come along.

"An ancient Indian burial ground," Marley explained. "We'll have to land quick so we have some daylight left."

Betsy sought Mother and asked permission to explore the big mound. Then she stood at the helm and waited for it to come into sight.

"Look," George said from right beside her. "It's steep."

"It's an eighty-degree angle," Betsy read from the *Navigator.* "It's seventy-five feet tall and one hundred eighty yards around the base."

"Can we climb it?"

Should they climb a grave? Betsy had always been careful

not to step on graves in the cemetery next to the churchyard back in Boston. It might be disrespectful to the Indians, and that might upset Marley. She didn't want to risk that.

As soon as the flatboat was secured for the night, Betsy, George, and Marley departed in the skiff and quickly reached ground.

"I'm going to the top," George shouted and took off.

Betsy glanced at Marley.

"Can't stop him," Marley said. "That's one curious boy. You can go look it over, if you want."

The mound was covered in trees. Betsy hiked up her dress and began the long climb, holding onto low branches for balance. George was halfway up. Marley stayed at the foot of the mound.

"It sounds hollow," George called down from his lofty perch. He was beating on the slanted ground with a downed branch.

The *Navigator* had said it sounded hollow, too, but Betsy couldn't detect that from the sound she heard. She rested against a very tall oak, then began the steep climb again. "It's caved in on top," George yelled back.

By the time Betsy reached the peak, George was down in the sinkhole, which was about four feet deep. Only his head peeked out of the deep basin. "I'm looking for some Indian stuff," he said, "but there's nothing here but more brush."

Betsy walked around the perimeter of the sinkhole. He was right—nothing there but brush. She looked off in the distance, searching the plain below for the ghost town that was mentioned in the guidebook. There it was, an old town that never took root once Wheeling was established. Only some old tumbled-down buildings remained. Odd. White man had tried to put a town here and failed where the Indians had declared the land a cemetery. The old white oak near the basin was a good four feet in diameter. How old did that make this mound? A hundred years? Two hundred years?

"Help me out, Betsy," George ordered.

Betsy's thoughts were pulled to her cousin who was trying unsuccessfully to climb out of the sinkhole.

"Now why would you climb in there if you didn't have a way out?" she asked. Here was a golden opportunity to embarrass him, and there was no one around to notice it.

"There aren't any footholds. Come on, give me a hand."

"Say please," she said.

"Betsy. Are you going to help me or not?"

She had to help him out, or Marley would climb that hill and get him out. "Say please," she said again.

"Please," George said finally.

Betsy knelt on the ground and reached for him with one arm while circling a tree as a brace with the other arm. George grabbed her hand and walked up the sinkhole wall.

"Thanks," he said grudgingly.

"You're welcome," she said with a tilt of her head. "Are you ready to go down? Marley's waiting."

The descent was as difficult as the climb because of the steep slope. Betsy inched her way, but George scampered down. When she was on level ground, Betsy discovered Marley had spent his waiting time gathering rocks and was placing them in the form of a cross at the foot of the mound.

Betsy began picking up some stones and put them in the formation. George helped. "Marley," Betsy said, "do you think the Indians buried here went to heaven? I mean, if they didn't know about the Lord, how could they be saved?"

That question had first crossed her mind when she read about the mounds.

"Well, missy, I don't rightly have an answer. I just don't know. That's one of the mysteries of God. I guess we'll find out soon enough."

"I guess we will," Betsy said.

They finished the cross in silence.

CHAPTER TEN
The Deserted House

On the fourth morning of the river journey, Betsy faced the stern of the flatboat and watched the Indian mound disappear from view. When she could no longer see it, she turned around and settled onto her usual crate seat. She consulted the maps to guess how far they would get that day.

The river curved past Big Grave Creek and churned in a narrows. The men hugged the right shore and got the flatboat through the ripples.

"I like the faster water," George said.

It was more adventurous, and Betsy was surprised to find that she also liked the ripples. "We're headed for Captina Island," she said. "Big curves coming up."

The river switched back on itself before it turned again to the southwest.

"Hey, look. Other travelers," George said.

Not only was there another flatboat ahead, it appeared to be stuck.

Betsy consulted the guide. "There's a sandbar at the lower end of the island and then two narrow channels with swift water. They must have snagged."

"Ahoy," Marley called to the stranded travelers.

Betsy could see two men and two women working on a portion of their boat. A couple of children sat on the roof.

"We've got a hole," one man called. "Hit a log."

"Have you got oakum?" Marley asked.

"No, we've used it all."

Marley looked at Father as if asking a question.

"Where can we tie up?" Father asked.

After some maneuvering, the men managed to get the boat in a position so it wouldn't float down the river or hang up on the close sandbar. The three men loaded mending supplies in the skiff and rowed upstream about fifty yards to the stranded flatboat.

Betsy watched them caulk the joints. George wandered into the covered area, then returned to where Betsy was sitting, carrying his family's shelf clock.

"What are you doing?" Betsy asked as he placed it on a high crate so the weights hung in the air.

"This wasn't keeping good time before we left Boston. I've going to fix it."

"What do you know about clocks?"

"I can learn," he said. He took the back off the clock and pulled on the weight, then pushed the pendulum so it would start. "This gear makes this gear turn, which makes this one turn the hands," he mumbled as if to himself. "If I turn this one, then this. . ."

"George, what are you doing with that clock?" his mother asked. She stood outside the flatboat house, looking as if this wasn't the first time she had caught George operating on something.

"I'm fixing it," he said. "It's been losing time."

"Do you know how?"

"I'm figuring it out," George said.

"Perhaps you'd better wait until your father can help you with it," Aunt Eleanor said. She had the patience of Job, Betsy decided. If George were her child. . .Well, that wouldn't bear thinking about.

George reluctantly carried the clock back into the covered area and returned with a lost look on his face.

"I wish we could go ashore again," he said.

"Well, we can't."

"I wish we could do something exciting."

"We are. We're floating down the Ohio River. Some people back home would think that was pretty exciting," Betsy said.

"Maybe. But being stuck on a boat all day and all night is downright confining."

A thought she'd had before. It was scary how she and George thought so much alike at times.

"I wish I could help those people. I could fix that boat. I helped put oakum on this boat."

"Quit wishing and do something," Betsy said.

"There's nothing to do."

"Then invent something," she said.

George mumbled something, then wandered away from what Betsy considered her area.

Betsy read her maps and saw no place of great interest coming up that day. There were several places they could stop and exercise Silverstreak, but Father might not want another delay.

With that in mind, Betsy walked along the narrow passage beside the covered area to the stern and untied Silverstreak.

"You only get to walk a few feet, then turn around," she said, "but it's better than nothing." Betsy quickly tired of the routine, but counted fifty turns before she tethered the horse.

Traveling down the river gave her different landscapes to view, but being tied up in one spot during the day was downright boring.

Betsy walked along the narrow passageway toward the front of the boat and glanced toward the stalled travelers. They were still working on the hole, but it looked like they were making progress.

Her foot stumbled on something, and she tried to regain her balance.

"No!" she screamed, and the next thing she knew, she was in the frigid water. She came up sputtering and grabbed for the boat, but missed before her heavy skirts took her down again. She bobbed back to the surface.

"Man overboard," George called.

The children on the roof of the flatboat house were screaming. Everyone on both boats was yelling at her, Marley louder than anyone.

"Splash with your hands. Kick your feet," he shouted. Betsy did her best, but back under the water she went.

She coughed when she resurfaced and beat the water with her hands, but down she went again. Each time she submerged, she seemed to go deeper and take longer to come up to the top.

"Betsy, give me your hand," Mother cried when Betsy came up yet again and gasped for air.

She quit splashing the water and reached for Mother, who was lying on the boat with her hand outstretched. But Betsy couldn't reach her.

"Grab this," George called and threw a rope that hit her in the head. Down she went once more, and this time she thought she would never breathe air again.

But she resurfaced, and this time she grabbed the rope, her lifeline. Mother and Aunt Eleanor and George pulled her toward the boat. With shaking hands Betsy gripped the wood, then climbed on the boat, with her mother pulling on her arms.

"Build up the fire," Mother ordered Aunt Eleanor. "Let's get these wet things off you, Betsy. Are you okay now? How did this happen? Did you lose your footing?"

Through chattering teeth, Betsy muttered, "I tripped on something." She pointed at the narrow passageway beside the covered house and saw string stretched across the walkway. She glared at George.

"You said invent something, so I invented a way I could catch three fish at once. See, I put hooks on three. . ."

"I don't want to hear it," Betsy interrupted as she lumbered in her soaking wet dress toward the covered area. She left a trail of water behind her.

Mother helped her peel her wet things off, and Betsy wrapped up in a blanket in front of the fire to get warm before donning dry clothes. She could hear Aunt Eleanor lecturing George on making sure his inventions didn't involve other people.

Betsy sat in front of the fire, finger-combing her hair, when the men rowed back to the boat.

"Are you all right, Betsy?" Father asked and hugged her tight.

"I'm cold," she said. "But it happened so fast. I'm okay now."

"That's my girl." He kissed her forehead. "Losing your brothers was bad enough, but I couldn't have stood to lose you," he said as if to himself.

"But you still wish I were a boy," Betsy said.

"Betsy, that's not true. Why would you think that?" Father tilted her chin up so she was looking at him.

"You're always talking to George, saying he's a curious boy."

"He is, and I like to encourage his questions because I want him to learn, but that doesn't mean I want you to be a boy. You're a wonderful girl, and you're going to be a magnificent woman.

"Did you hit your head when you fell into the water?" he asked with a smile. He kissed her forehead again. "You're precious to me. Never forget that."

Betsy felt a lurch as the boat was untied and the journey

was underway again.

"I'd better take my position with the sweep. We fixed those folks up and got them off the sandbar. They're going to wait for the oakum to cure a bit, then they'll move along. Want to go sit in the sun?"

"Not yet," Betsy said. "I'll stay here by the fire a little longer." Physically, she felt chilled to the bone and couldn't bring herself to leave the heat of the fire. But her heart felt warmer and lighter.

Before noon, Betsy took up her normal post with the guidebook. George stayed out of her way once he had mumbled sorry and something about making sure he didn't endanger anyone again.

Betsy just nodded and didn't look up from her book. She tried to search for landmarks the book mentioned, but she couldn't concentrate on the words or the shoreline. She trembled as she stared into the Ohio River that churned along beside her. That last time she had gone under, the river had swallowed her. She'd opened her eyes and seen nothing but water, still muddied from the spring flood. Panic set in.

"How are you doing?" Marley stepped toward her from his post with the long oar. He still watched ahead, but withdrew his sweep from the water.

"I'm all right," Betsy said.

"A bit scared?" he asked and nodded, answering his own question. "And rightly so."

"It was dark under the water," she said. "And I was so helpless."

"I know. I was in there once," he said. His eyes looked misty, and he moved back to his post.

Betsy closed her eyes. "Dear God," she whispered. "Thank You for getting me out of the river. Please help me not be scared anymore. Amen." A tear trickled down her cheek, and she wiped it off and took a deep breath.

The rest of the day Betsy sat on her crate. When they docked, she felt much better, but she didn't leave the boat with George and Marley when they took the skiff to shore. There wasn't much to see anyway. That night she dreamed she was under the water again and woke up, gasping for air.

Two more days of travel brought them to Marietta, where they tied up at a wharf.

"Tonight we sleep in real beds," Father said. "Tomorrow is Sunday, and we're taking a day of rest."

The tired travelers unloaded a few bags and found rooms at an inn. Silverstreak was boarded at a stable. On Sunday morning after a breakfast where they sat at a real table, they attended church. Father and Mother visited easily with the townspeople. Betsy smiled at a couple of girls and said hello when they greeted her as they walked by. Odd. In the past she would have been too shy to speak to strangers.

In the afternoon they walked around the town and were glad to get the exercise. Betsy rode Silverstreak, and George threw sticks on the town square for Jefferson to fetch.

"There's a shipbuilding yard here," Uncle Paul said at dinner.

Betsy looked up from her plate of ham and potatoes. Did that mean Uncle Paul might want to stay in Marietta? She liked the town and wouldn't mind it if they stayed here.

"I noticed that, too," Father said. "But there are several

shipyards in Cincinnati."

"Yes, and someday a yard will have my name on it," Uncle Paul said.

"We'll shove off tomorrow morning after the women have time to visit the market and lay in some fresh supplies," Father said.

It was midmorning before they boarded the flatboat again. Betsy felt better after spending time ashore. She could face the Ohio again without the trepidation that had haunted her.

She took up her old post with her maps and the *Navigator* and read the pages about the next few miles.

"Marley," she said excitedly. "Will we get to the Blennerhassett mansion before nightfall?"

"Yes, Missy. With our late start this morning, I suspect that's where we'll spend the night. There's a stone boat landing where we can tie up real easy."

"Oh, can we go ashore? Can we see the house?"

"It was once a grand place," Marley said. "But last spring a crest of floodwater drowned the gardens and filled the house."

"Have you seen it since?"

"Yes. It's but a ghost of its former self."

"Ghost?" George had edged over by Marley. "What ghost?"

Betsy ignored him. "Where are the owners?" she asked Marley.

"I don't know. All I know are rumors. Aaron Burr was involved with Mr. Blennerhassett in some movement to take New Orleans by force and form a new government there. Both were arrested, and I don't know the outcome of it. Meanwhile the house has been ransacked and left deserted."

"Vice President Aaron Burr?" Betsy asked.

"He was the vice president. Now we have a different one."

"I know. Clinton," Betsy said, remembering that Thomas Jefferson had changed vice presidents for his second term.

"Where is this place?" George asked.

Betsy looked at her map. "About eight more miles. We'll get there before dark."

"I'll ask if we can explore it," George said and disappeared inside the covered area.

"Do you know anything else about the place?" Betsy asked Marley.

"Blennerhassett was quite a curious fellow," the man said. "I never met him, but I heard that he played the cello and did all sorts of experiments trying to invent things."

"Like George," Betsy said.

"Much like George," Marley agreed. "But I think the lad means well."

"What about Mrs. Blennerhassett?"

"I understand she was quite pretty. They had a couple sons."

"Did she play a musical instrument?" Betsy asked, thinking that perhaps the woman had played the violin.

"I never heard anything like that," Marley said. "Although I heard they had some big parties. Half of what's said about them is probably untrue. When people are so wealthy and fall on hard times, there's usually a lot of tales spread about them."

"How much farther?" George asked. " We can go ashore, but we have to be careful, and Marley has to go, too."

"I'd like to see the place again," Marley said.

It was nearing sundown when the travelers approached the east end of the biggest island in the Ohio.

"The other end is owned by someone else," Betsy explained to George. "We must be careful to stay on the deserted side."

Tying up at the stone wharf was as easy as Marley had said, and the threesome jumped off the boat onto the dock.

They walked up a path that was still silt-covered from the flood and ambled toward the two-story house. From the back Betsy could see honeysuckle vines on a trellis next to the house. At least the vines had survived the dunking by the Ohio River.

One-story curving wings flanked both sides of the two-story main part of the house. Even in its deserted state, the mansion remained graceful.

"I'm going to walk down where the orchards were and see if any of the trees have greened up," Marley said. "I'll be back in a moment."

Betsy and George stared at the house. In the fading sunlight, it took on a ghostly air, and that thought gave Betsy an idea.

"I wonder if the old place is haunted. I've heard there are lots of rumors about it. Are you afraid to go in there?" Betsy asked.

"Of course not," George scoffed.

"Go on in. I dare you to climb upstairs and wave from the window."

George glanced around. "Where did Marley go?"

"Down that path. He'll be right back. Afraid?"

George didn't answer but strode toward the front door that stood ajar. When he reached the verandah, his pace slowed. He glanced over his shoulder at Betsy, then stepped on the porch. He glanced back one more time before he disappeared.

CHAPTER ELEVEN
Marley's Secret

Her plan was simply to scare George as much as her fall into the Ohio River because of his fishing invention had scared her. He needed to know how his actions affected other people, she decided.

With lightning speed, she raced to the house, then tiptoed up the step to the verandah. Cautiously, she peered inside the doorway. There was no sign of George. Maybe he was already on the staircase.

She sneaked into the house. Once her eyes were accustomed to the dimness within, she could make out heaps of broken furniture in the large room to her left. Above her the chandelier in the entry hung without one glass globe left intact. A lone candle sat in its holder.

The floor was covered with silt and sand. As she stepped carefully into the next room, she noticed many footprints, as if other travelers had stopped to see the former splendor of the mansion. So this was where Mr. Blennerhassett had played the cello. She could imagine herself standing over by the ornate mantel of the fireplace, playing Richard's violin. Dozens of friends would dance to the sweet music in the large room. What a party they would have, and what an odd thought. She didn't play the violin in front of others. Until this trip, she'd only played for Richard and for Mother and Father. Now George's family and Marley had heard her, too.

Above her, she heard George's halting footsteps. She had to act fast. What could she do to make an eerie sound? To her left were broken parts of a rocking chair. She picked up two wooden pieces that must have formed rungs and struck one with the other, making a knocking sound. The footsteps upstairs stopped, and Betsy smiled. She tapped on the wall three times, then repeated the code three more times.

"Betsy," George called from upstairs.

She didn't answer.

"Betsy, is that you?" His voice was quavering now.

She said nothing but instead pounded on the wall with her fist. That movement jarred jagged pieces of a large broken mirror that clung to a frame, and they fell to the floor. Betsy jumped, and the tinkling of breaking glass echoed through the house. A scream came from upstairs.

"Good," she whispered. She silently glided to the staircase and climbed, step by step. She didn't try to mask the noise of the creaky stairs, and for good measure, she moaned as she climbed up and up.

Running footsteps made for the back of the house. With her long legs, Betsy took two steps at a time and quickly reached the second floor. She could hear George scurrying toward the back of the house, and she ran to the first door across from the stairs. The room was empty except for trashed furniture. What had possessed someone to tear up such a grand bed? She started for the second door and knew this was where George was. She could hear whimpering sounds.

She jumped into the second room and yelled, "Boo!"

George was on the window ledge, ready to jump. Betsy watched him grab the trellis beside the window and swing out. She dashed to the window and peered out at the same time that she heard the sound of splintering wood. The trellis was pulling away from the house.

"George!" she screamed.

Her cousin yelled in terror.

Betsy stretched out the window and grabbed the trellis, bringing George back toward the house. "Can you climb back in?"

"No, there's something in there!"

"What's going on?" Marley ran around the corner of the house and reached the base of the trellis.

"Can you help George down?" Betsy called. Her arms ached from holding the trellis in place. She didn't know how much longer she could retain her grip. With Marley's guidance, George inched his way down the trellis, his weight pulling the trellis from the house as Betsy struggled to keep it close. Finally he was on the ground, and she let go.

"Look out," she cried as the wooden structure crashed to the ground.

"Get out, Betsy," George shouted. "There's something up there." He whirled toward Marley. "We have to get her out before it gets her."

Betsy didn't wait to hear anymore. She ran for the stairs. If George had been hurt, it would have been her fault. And here he was wanting to come back in to save her. She bounded down the stairs and out the front door in time to see George and Marley come around the left wing of the house. She ran toward them.

"Did you see anything?" George asked. "Did you hear anything?"

"I heard a mirror break," she said, trying to catch her breath. She didn't admit that she'd accidentally broken it when she pounded on the wall.

"I heard it, too. Let's get back to the boat." When she didn't move, George added insistently, "Now! That house is haunted."

"There's no such thing as a ghost," Marley said. "There's a logical explanation for whatever you heard." He looked hard at Betsy. She looked away.

"In any event," Marley added, "we do need to get back to the boat. It'll be dark in a few minutes."

"It moaned, too," George said, "and it made a knocking sound in a rhythm, as if it was trying to say something."

"It was probably the wind," Marley said, "making a branch tap against the wall of the house." Again he looked at Betsy.

"What about the orchard?" she asked.

"It's gone. The trees were too young to survive. The power of nature, the floodwaters, were too much for them." His voice trembled, and now it was Betsy's turn to look searchingly at him.

Once they were back on the boat, George recounted the excitement in the house.

"There are no such things as ghosts," Uncle Paul told his son.

Father agreed with him. "It was your imagination playing tricks on you."

"But Betsy heard the mirror break, too," George protested.

"A mirror?" Marley said in a low voice that only Betsy could hear. "Not just a piece of glass?"

Betsy turned away and stared at the water.

After dinner, while the others were inside the shelter, out of the cool wind that had sprung up, Betsy made her way to the back of the boat to check on Silverstreak.

"Why?"

Betsy jumped at the sound of Marley's voice.

"I didn't hear you come out here," she said in a husky voice.

"Why did you scare George?" Marley asked.

Betsy bit her lip, then sighed. "I wanted to scare him as much as I was scared when I fell in the river."

"He didn't mean to harm you, and you meant to scare him."

"I know. And if he'd been hurt it would have been my fault." She felt tears slip down her cheeks. She should confess what she'd done, apologize to George. She knew that, but wasn't it too late?

"You were very scared in the water," Marley said. "I know the power of the river. I know your fear."

"How could you know my fear?" Betsy lashed out. "It was so dark."

He didn't answer for a long while.

"My wife and my baby daughter and I were caught in floodwaters."

Betsy stood up straighter. Some instinct told her what was coming next.

"Our boat was stove in by trees hidden under the water. She went down in seconds."

"And your wife and daughter?"

"Drowned, I guess. . ." His voice broke off. He sniffed, then continued. "I never found them. I searched for months. Their bodies never washed ashore."

"Oh, Marley, I'm so sorry," Betsy choked out. She laid her head against the horse's neck and cried.

"I wanted revenge," Marley said. "I wanted God to tell me why I was alive and they were dead. I was thrown into a submerged treetop, and it held me above the water. I cursed the rain and the floodwaters. Why did God take my family from me?"

109

"Do you know why?" Betsy asked on a sob.

"No. They went to heaven, of that I'm sure."

Betsy cried quietly into the mare's mane until she regained control. "So that's the tragedy in your life," she said.

"Yes. Moon Silver and little Sarah are now memories to me, and I think of them every day."

"Moon Silver? She was an Indian?"

"Yes. I lived in her settlement for two years. We were headed west when the boat sank. I returned here to tell her family. And I started taking others down the river. I had to tame the river. Prove to myself that I could take families safely down. But I always wait until the spring flood has passed. I warn other families of the dangers of the flood-waters, but few listen to me."

"So that's why you hadn't already gone down the river when we needed a guide."

"Yes. Now I've told you my story. I understand how afraid you were of the water. But was scaring George the way to handle your fear?"

Betsy looked out at the black night. The flickering light from the lantern inside the enclosure left deep shadows. She couldn't see the water, but she could hear it rush by.

"If I'd looked at my feet, I would have seen the string and not tripped. George shouldn't have put it in the way, but it wasn't exactly his fault. I should apologize?" She asked the question, but she knew the answer. They made their way back to the group inside the shelter. Betsy sat down beside George.

"I made the sounds in the mansion. I'm sorry," she said without preamble.

"You were the ghost?" George said in a loud voice. The

110

others stopped talking.

"Betsy?" Mother said.

"I-I wanted to get George back for making me fall in the river. I wanted to scare him, but I know that was wrong. I'm sorry." She tried to hold back the tears, but the last few moments had been too emotional for her.

"I forgive you," George said. "I shouldn't have put the string in the walkway."

Betsy waited for Mother to chastise her, but no one else spoke for a moment.

"Now that that's taken care of, I think I'll turn in," Marley said. His statement ended the evening, and Betsy cast him a grateful look.

In the morning, nothing more was said of the mansion or of Betsy's trick, and she sighed with relief as she took up her post with the *Navigator*.

The last few days had been unseasonably warm. For several days Betsy had sat on her crate seat without her cloak around her, but this day was different. By noon, the wind came up and the sky darkened with huge black clouds.

"We'd best be finding a place to hole up," Marley said. "The sooner the better."

Betsy consulted her maps and found several places that might work, but the first three were already taken by other flatboaters. They waved as they floated by, searching for the next place.

They hadn't seen much river traffic going downriver, since it all seemed to be floating at the same rate. But now they discovered just how many other travelers shared the river with them.

George and Betsy made a lean-to shelter out of canvas to cover Silverstreak, and George insisted that Jefferson be allowed inside their little house.

Rain was already pelting down by the time they found a cove where they could tie up for the night. The women fed the fire in the covered area while the men secured the boat. Rain fell hard and steadily throughout the night. By morning it hadn't slackened any.

"We're staying put," Father said. They sat inside the shelter, peering out when an adventurous flatboater would float past. Betsy read in the dim light from the fire and kept pushing Jefferson away. That smelly dog wanted to be close to the fire, too.

Once Marley and Father rowed ashore and found more wood to keep the fire going. By nightfall the rain showed no sign of abating, but by morning, it was a gentle rain, and Father and Uncle Paul and Marley rowed the flatboat out of its safe berth and into the current of the Ohio again.

"We must keep a sharp eye," Marley said. "The sand shifts after a heavy rain." Although the men watched, and Betsy read aloud from the *Navigator* about where the sandbars were located, by late morning the flatboat caught on a newly formed sandbar.

"Push off! Push off!" Marley yelled. The men strained against their sweeps. Betsy held her breath as they pushed to no avail.

"Move these crates starboard," Marley said. "The weight on that side should raise this side, and we can push it off again."

Betsy and the others hurried to do his bidding, and although the right side of the flatboat tipped dangerously close to water level, with lots of grunts and muscle power, the men were able to free the boat from the sand's hold.

George and Betsy and the women scurried to move the crates back to even out the load on the boat, and it once again found the river's current and floated downstream.

Everyone was wet, and once the rain stopped for good, the travelers changed into dry clothes.

"We'll make clotheslines out of these ropes," George said, and Betsy helped him string rope across the boat.

"We look like a Monday washing day back home," Mother said once they hung all the clothes out for the sun to dry.

Back home. It had been days since Betsy had wondered about Mary and the ships in Boston Harbor and if Richard had returned from the sea. A wave of intense homesickness washed over her. It was as dark as the waters of the Ohio River.

CHAPTER TWELVE
The Hold Up

The next few days fell into a pattern. Good weather returned, and with it, traffic on the river increased.

"Why didn't we see other boats before?" Betsy asked. "It seems every day we see more and more."

"At first we must have been traveling at about the same speed," Marley answered. "So the only travelers we saw were the ones who were stranded or keelboats that were going upriver. Some of these boats are merchant boats. They stop fairly often so we can overtake them."

Not only did they overtake them, Mother bought goods from one merchant. He sold a bit of everything, and Mother even found a book to add to Betsy's collection.

They also started stopping at wharves when it wasn't time to stop for the night. Father said Silverstreak would lose muscle tone if she wasn't exercised each day, so they took the opportunity to unload the horse at least once a day.

On the evenings when they tied up at a settlement's wharf, there would be other boats tied there. Occasionally in the coves where they'd stay for the night there would be others, too. Once they all went ashore and shared dinner with another family. They sat around a campfire, and when Father suggested that Betsy get her violin, she complied.

These were friendly folks, and she doubted that she would ever see them again, so she struck up a tune and they sang along.

Some days Betsy and George guessed how many boats they would see along the way. Keelboats counted, too.

"At least we've never been passed by a flatboat," George said. "We've got a pretty fast boat."

"Yes," Marley said, "and a sturdy one. The extra time your father took working on this boat has made it hold up when a lesser boat would have sprung a leak."

"My father's going to own his own boatyard soon," George said proudly.

"Yes, and it will be a quality outfit," Marley replied.

Jefferson barked, which usually meant he heard wildlife along the shore or more river traffic.

Betsy heard the noise before they rounded the bend in the river and came upon two boats fastened together near the middle of the channel. The noise almost drowned out her words.

"What is it?"

"A sawmill," Marley said. "That paddlewheel between the boats powers the saw." He called directions to Father and Uncle Paul, and they steered the boat to the left of the floating sawmill.

Late that afternoon they tied the boat at a rickety dock near the mouth of Salt Creek. The three men were busy applying oakum to the stern. Uncle Paul had noticed a place that might be a potential trouble spot.

"Best to take care of it before we spring a leak," he said.

"What about Silverstreak?" Betsy asked her mother. "Can I take her for a ride without Marley? There are some fields on the other side of the trees, and there's even a salt lick not far from here." She had just read about it in the guide. "That must be why this dock is here."

Mother scanned the shoreline. "It looks all right, I guess. But take George and Jefferson, too."

Betsy hadn't exactly avoided George since the episode at the Blennerhassett mansion, but she hadn't sought him out, either. Now she called to him and asked if he wanted to go ashore. She knew what his response would be. Within a few minutes Betsy and George were ashore. They followed a narrow path, with George and Jefferson staying way behind Silverstreak.

"I'm going to look for the salt lick," George said when they came to a point where the wooded path forked. He tugged on the rope that was tied to Jefferson, and they headed west while Betsy turned Silverstreak in the opposite direction.

"I'll be back in a little while," she said. "Stay out of trouble.

We'll go back to the boat together." A little way past the woods that fronted the river, a wide field opened up. Betsy let Silverstreak canter. The mare threw her head up and raced through the new green grass. If she didn't know better, Betsy would have said the horse grinned at having freedom of movement again.

They'd been on the river for fifteen days. They were all tired, but Marley said they should reach Cincinnati in another four days on the outside. Three if everything went well. She didn't know what lay in store for them in Cincinnati, but she was ready for a real home with a real address. Then she could write to Mary again and hope for a letter in return.

April wildflowers dotted the pasture to her right, and she rode among the blues and yellows and sweet scents of the early flowers. Perhaps she and Mother could put out flowers at their new home. She could transplant wildflowers, and there would be many more to choose from in May.

To her left was a dogwood in full bloom. She rode under the tree, ducking so she wouldn't get hit by the low branches, then she stopped Silverstreak and sat up straight. It was as if she were a part of the tree. To her left, to her right, below her, and above her were the fragrant white blossoms.

She breathed in deeply and sat still a few moments until Silverstreak neighed. When the mare reared her head, she hit a branch, so Betsy carefully guided her out from under the tree.

The sun was getting low, and she knew she should find George and return to the confinement of the boat. With a sigh, she turned away from the lovely tree and headed back in the direction she had come.

George was nowhere to be seen. She whistled, thinking Jefferson might respond with a bark, but nothing. Once she reached the fork in the wooded path, she rode west over a mile, toward where she suspected the salt lick was located, but she didn't see George. He probably couldn't have covered that much ground on foot in the time she'd been riding Silverstreak. Where could that boy and his dog have gotten to?

Leave it to George to get lost the one time they were trusted enough to go ashore alone. She turned Silverstreak toward the river and slowly headed back through the woods toward the flatboat. Glancing left and right, she searched for George and Jefferson. She found him hiding behind a big tree about two hundred yards from the river.

Before she could say a word, he held his finger to his lips for silence. The alarmed expression on his face made her bite back the words that rose to her lips. She turned Silverstreak around and rode her back up the path, then tied her to a tree. Gingerly Betsy walked toward George, who was still staring at her with huge eyes.

She tiptoed to his hiding place.

"What are you doing?" she whispered.

"There's a strange man on the boat," George whispered back.

"Probably just another traveler."

"I don't think so. Look!"

Betsy peeked around the side of the tree at the boat. It was a good two hundred yards down to the water's edge, and she couldn't see details clearly, but the stance of the men signaled danger. Father, Uncle Paul, and Marley faced the man. Mother and Aunt Eleanor hovered near the opening to the covered area.

"What are they doing?" George asked.

"I don't know." She saw the setting sun reflect off something in the stranger's hand. Betsy gasped. "I think he's got a gun."

"Is he robbing them?"

"We've got to do something. He might hurt them."

"What can we do?" George asked.

"Let me think. Did you find the salt lick? Did you see any men there?"

"No, I didn't get that far. Jefferson chased a squirrel, and I had to chase him."

"So there's no help there. If we run down to the boat, he'll see us and that won't do any good."

"We need to catch him by surprise and tie him up," George whispered. Betsy nodded. She looked around for another boat or a little skiff, but their flatboat was the only one on the river.

"How do you suppose he got here? Afoot?" Betsy asked in a hushed whisper.

"Must have. He'll have to come up the path, won't he?"

"He should. Where's Jefferson?"

"I tied him to a tree back there," he motioned through the woods, but off the path. "Once I saw that man, I didn't want Jefferson barking. Look!"

Father was handing the man something, probably money they had saved to start over in Cincinnati. The man stuffed it in a bag and waved the gun around. Betsy could hear him speak, but she couldn't make out the words. From his arm motions, she guessed he was telling them to stay on the boat.

119

"Can you get Jefferson's rope without making him bark?" she asked. "Maybe we can trip him. One of us on each side of the path, and we'll jerk it up when he passes."

Without saying a word, George sneaked back into the woods. A couple minutes later he was back with the rope.

"I told Jefferson to stay."

"He's leaving," Betsy whispered. "Give me that end." She silently crawled across the path and hid behind a large oak. Leaning back into the trail, she covered the rope with some leaves, cringing when they made a rustling sound. George buried the rope on his side of the path.

"When he gets to this spot, pull on it," Betsy said.

She peeked around the tree and saw the man jump off the dock and bolt toward them. He wasn't fifty feet away when Jefferson barked. That dog again! The robber paused a second and cocked his head as if listening. Jefferson barked again, and this time the sound was farther away. He was probably chasing another squirrel. The man seemed satisfied that nothing was coming his way and scurried forward.

Betsy held her breath as she listened to the man's running steps crackle the leaves that littered the path. He came closer, closer. When he was almost upon them, she glanced across the path at George. He was staring at her, his huge eyes the only thing she noticed on his face.

"Now!" Betsy yelled, and they both jerked on the rope.

The man let out a curse as he fell. Before he could struggle to his feet, George jumped on his back, and Betsy wound the rope around his legs. The man shook George off, but when he finally managed to stand, the rope made him stumble again, and down he went.

"Get him," Betsy shouted and jumped on his back along with George.

"Betsy! George!" Father called. The three men came running up the sloping path.

Marley reached them first and pounced on the man. Father tied the man's hands behind his back with one end of the rope, leaving the other end wound around his legs.

Then Father grabbed Betsy and held her close. "We were so frightened that he would find you out here," he said.

"We got him good," George bragged.

"You sure did," Uncle Paul assured his son as he hugged him.

Marley picked up the bag the robber had carried. "I believe we'll be taking this back." He reached inside the man's coat and pulled out the gun. "I don't believe you'll be needing this where you're going." He turned to the other two men. "We can turn him over to the law in Adamsville."

"I'll get Silverstreak," Betsy said and explained where he was tied up. "I'll be just a minute."

The men hustled the prisoner back down the path to the boat.

"Jefferson," George called. He whistled, but there was no sound from the woods. "Jefferson!"

"Which way do you think he went?" Betsy asked.

"Back toward the salt lick, I think," George said and started up the path.

"Hop on and we'll find him," Betsy said.

"I'll walk," George said.

"Suit yourself." Betsy moved ahead on Silverstreak and called for Jefferson. Who would have thought she'd have to be looking for that dog? But George had captured the robber by getting Jefferson's rope and setting the dog free. It was the least she could do.

At the fork in the path, Betsy turned toward the west. "Jefferson," she called. As soon as the woods gave way to clear fields, Betsy urged Silverstreak into a canter. If George and Jefferson had come here before, it seemed logical that the dog would return, unless something else or some other animal claimed his attention.

Soon she could no longer hear George yelling and whistling back in the woods. The sun was nearly down. Riding in the dark on unknown ground was dangerous. A mile later, she turned the horse around and retraced her steps, although she still hadn't found the dog.

She saw George walking along the edge of the woods, still whistling and calling for his dog.

"We have to get back to the boat," Betsy told him.

"But Jefferson's out here somewhere."

"We'll find him tomorrow, first thing. Hurry, it's getting darker by the minute. Jefferson's a smart dog. He'll be all right."

George yelled for his dog all the way back to the boat, but there was no tale-tell barking in response. He lumbered onto the boat. The eyes that had been saucer-sized an hour earlier were now small with pain. Betsy knew how she'd feel if it had been Silverstreak out there alone, and she patted George on the back.

"We'll find him tomorrow," she said and explained to the others that they hadn't found the dog.

"He'll get hungry and come looking for us," Aunt Eleanor

told her son.

Betsy groomed Silverstreak, then joined the family for prayer before another meal of beans.

"Thank you, God, for delivering us from evil," Father ended grace. "And please help us find Jefferson, so that we may reward him for giving us his rope."

The prisoner was tied to a post on the side opposite the dock. Father untied his hands so he could eat, then retied them.

"Jefferson," George called toward shore every few minutes.

In desperation to get him to stop yelling, Betsy pulled out her violin. Jefferson had always howled when he heard her play. She'd thought of him as a bad critic, one more strike against him, but Father had explained that dogs seemed to hear high pitches better than people, and that he probably liked the high notes she reached.

She played songs with high clear notes and was about to put away the violin for the night when she heard a bark from the woods.

"Jefferson!" she said.

George must have heard him, too. He was already on his feet and reaching for the lantern. Uncle Paul followed his son.

"Jefferson," George called. He whistled for his dog as he jumped off the boat onto the dock. "Here, boy."

Betsy could hear the dog rustling leaves as he bounded down the path, barking and yelping. She struck up another tune, and Jefferson started his howling.

A few moments later a triumphant George returned to the boat carrying the little dog. Uncle Paul followed right behind him with the lantern.

"Don't you ever run away from me again," George lectured his dog. "We were all worried about you."

Not all of us, Betsy thought out of habit, then hastily amended that thought. She had been worried about the dog because he meant so much to George.

"Thank you, God, for returning him safely," she whispered.

Chapter Thirteen

Stuck!

Early the next morning the travelers floated down to Adamsville, where the men rowed the prisoner to shore. Father had assured Betsy that all their cash was safe now, and that the money hadn't been as important as the lives of his family.

"I was terrified that robber would find you and George in the woods," Mother said. "But I guess I didn't have to worry about you two. You worked together. I'm proud of that, Betsy."

Betsy nodded. She really hadn't thought about working with George. It had just happened.

Once the men returned to the boat, they cast off again, and Betsy took up her usual post with her maps.

"If we travel late this evening, we can make it to Limestone Creek, can't we?" Betsy asked Marley. The sun was staying up a little later each day, and she wanted to claim those few minutes as travel time.

"We might be tying up in the dark," he said, "but that's a big landing. There are bound to be lanterns out."

By dark, they were still on the river, determined to make it around the bend to Maysville on the Limestone. An hour later they tied up at the landing, one of several boats secured there. Father exercised Silverstreak on the main street, and the next morning they shoved off at sunrise.

"How far can we get today?" George asked after they had breakfasted on the river.

"If we can get to Bullskin Creek tonight," Betsy said, consulting her maps, "we might be able to make it to Cincinnati by tomorrow night."

"Two more days!" George exclaimed. His excitement matched Betsy's as they pushed on down the river. Even the adults caught the contagious fever of journey's end. They made good time, and by early afternoon they were nearing Bracken Creek.

"Stay port side," Marley called from the roof where he was steering the boat with his wide sweep. Father left his position on the left side and crossed to push off with Paul.

"Push! I can see the sandbar," Marley called. "It's farther out."

But they couldn't move in time, and the boat snagged on the bar, stopping so suddenly, Betsy slid off her perch on the crate. Marley had squatted on the roof, but Father and Uncle Paul both fell on the deck. Inside the shelter, Mother and Aunt Eleanor screamed as crates came crashing to the floor. Jefferson howled, and Silverstreak whinnied.

"Wow," George said. He was sprawled on the deck near Betsy's feet.

"Are you all right, Maggie?" Father quickly gained his stance and ran inside the enclosure. He appeared a moment later at the doorway. "We have a few displaced items, but nothing major. Anyone hurt?"

Betsy rubbed her arm that had scraped along the crate, but didn't say anything. She made her way down the narrow aisle beside the enclosure and settled Silverstreak.

"Let's get her off the bar," Marley called. "Any leaks?"

"None here," Uncle Paul called from aft. He examined the boat and declared it seaworthy. Then the work began.

The travelers stacked their heavy belongings on the freed side of the boat, so the side that was buried in the sandbar could be shoved loose.

They pushed, pulled, and tugged, but the flatboat remained still. Another flatboat passed by them, careful to stay on the far left, away from the grabbing sandbar.

"Can we help?" A bargeman from a keelboat called a few minutes later. This boat was making its way up the Ohio and was positioned below them.

Marley quickly conferred with the men on the keelboat,

and they threw a rope to the flatboat.

"They'll try to pull us out. If they stay in the channel, the current will help. Get ready to push."

All three men pushed off the sandbar with their long sweeps. On the keelboat, some bargemen pulled on the rope and others pushed on their long poles. The flatboat rocked and at last was freed from the sandbar.

Betsy and the others quickly redistributed the weight of the crates, Marley untied the rope, and the bargeman pulled it aboard the keelboat.

"Many thanks," Father called to them.

"Think nothing of it," the bargeman called.

"That was nice of them to help us," George said as they got underway again. "But why didn't that other boat stop?"

"It wasn't the Christian thing to do," Betsy said, "going by us like that."

"There could have been many reasons," Mother said. "It's not for us to judge what's in the hearts of others."

"Does this mean we won't get to Cincinnati tomorrow?" George asked.

Betsy glanced at the sun, but Marley answered before she could estimate the distance and the hours of sunlight left.

"This delay has cost us dearly in time. We'll spend two more days on the river," he said, "but that will let us get to Cincinnati in the daylight instead of at night. That will make it easier."

Perhaps, Betsy thought, but she had hoped that this would be her last night of sleeping on the boat.

By the next evening, excitement aboard the boat was a

tangible thing. George skipped along the deck; Betsy's violin had never had a happier voice; and Jefferson barked at every bird along the shore. They anchored near Little Indian Creek, and Betsy had a hard time falling asleep.

At daybreak, the travelers cast off for the last time. By afternoon, George was dancing across the boat, and Betsy was calling off each landmark they passed.

"That's Little Miami River," Betsy said. "It's not far now." She stood on her crate, as if that bit of additional height could make her see farther.

George stood at the bow. "Look," he shouted a few minutes later. "Cincinnati!"

Mother and Aunt Eleanor stood beside Betsy and stared at the shoreline. Dwelling after dwelling came into sight. It wasn't the size of Boston, but it was the biggest town they had seen since they left Pittsburgh.

"We're home," Mother said, "at last."

"Home?" Betsy echoed. Not home. Boston was home. They were in Cincinnati.

"Yes, home," Mother said, in a voice that brooked no argument. "This is our home now." Betsy didn't reply, but her excitement at finally arriving dimmed.

They docked and unloaded Silverstreak. Father tied her to a hitching post while they walked to a public house on the main street. As soon as they had washed up and drank a refreshing cup of tea, Father turned to Betsy.

"Take Silverstreak to the stable and arrange for her board." He handed her several coins.

"You want me to go alone?" she asked.

"Yes, please. The innkeeper said Potter's Stable is a few

blocks farther down this street, but on a corner, so it faces north."

"But, Father, you want me to talk to the man at the stable?"

"Yes, Betsy. I need to arrange for storage for our movings and get them off the boat this afternoon. Take George with you."

"But I can help you," George protested.

"Yes, you can. After you help Betsy with Silverstreak," Father said.

Betsy and Marley walked side by side toward the boat, while George raced with Jefferson to the river.

"You have a problem with the horse?" Marley asked.

"No," Betsy replied. "I have a problem talking to strangers."

"Now I never noticed that," Marley said. "You took right up with me."

"You're different," Betsy said.

"No. I'm the same as everyone else. Give people a chance, Betsy. They're just like you and me."

She nodded but didn't reply. She'd taken up with Marley because Father had said he had overcome tragedy and she should be nice to him. He didn't seem like a threat to her. Surely everyone hadn't overcome tragedy. But could there be something in their lives that they struggled with, too?

They arrived at the post where Silverstreak was hitched, and Betsy untied her.

"Come on, George," she called.

"I'm coming," he said, but stayed a good ten feet behind her with Jefferson yapping at his feet as they made their way back down the main street.

Once they passed the inn, Betsy scrutinized each corner, looking for the stable. Four streets later she found it.

"You want to talk to the man?" she called back to George, who still lagged behind.

"You do it, but hurry up so we can get back to the boat. They've probably already found a place to store our movings and are unloading."

Betsy stood outside the stable and looked into the dim interior. Stalls lined both sides of the barnlike structure. She could make out a figure near the back.

"Come hold Silverstreak," she ordered George, as she mustered her courage to go inside. She had done this in Pittsburgh, but Silverstreak's keep had already been arranged, and it was a boy she'd talked with. She'd known that they'd be leaving town shortly, so it didn't matter what the stable boy thought of her.

"No. Tie her up," George said from the street.

A couple boys about George's age walked around the corner. "Why are you afraid of Silverstreak? Are you afraid of all horses?" she asked in exasperation. The two boys snickered as they walked by, and George turned a brilliant shade of red.

Betsy stared at him. He was embarrassed. She'd tried so many ways to embarrass him that hadn't worked and then out of the blue, she'd done it. It didn't feel as good as she had thought it would. An eye for an eye, that was her purpose: to humiliate him the way he'd humiliated her. But this vengeance didn't sit well with her. Turning the other cheek was much more her philosophy. Why hadn't she seen that before?

She turned and walked purposefully into the stable, leading the mare.

"I have a horse to board," she said to the man, who was walking toward her. "Dr. Thomas Miller is the owner, and her name is Silverstreak. I'll be exercising her most days. What's the charge?"

He named an amount, and she paid him a week's board.

She led Silverstreak into the stall the man pointed out, and promised the horse she'd return later that day to ride her.

"When you come back, I'll tell you the best roads to take," the man offered.

"Thank you," she said. He had been quite nice. Maybe Marley was right, and she needed to give others a chance instead of being too shy to speak.

By the time Betsy and George arrived at the river, Father, Uncle Paul, and Marley were unloading the boat and putting the crates on a flatbed wagon.

"We're headed to the river warehouse," Father said, and motioned to a nearby building. "Not far to move our things, and from the looks of the clouds, we'd better hurry."

Betsy glanced up and watched dark clouds soar across the sky. There was strong wind up high, but on the ground the wind wasn't nearly as fierce.

The rain held off until nightfall, and by that time all the Millers' and Langfords' belongings were safe and dry in the warehouse. Father, Uncle Paul, and Marley had found a place to anchor the flatboat so that it could be torn apart for the lumber to start on the houses.

"First we'll build ours," Father said when the two families gathered around the dinner table at the inn. "Then we'll all live there until we can get Paul's up. We'll find a suitable place tomorrow."

"And I'll be finding a keelboat that wants another hand," Marley said.

Betsy gasped, surprised that he was leaving. Yet she'd known that he was hired to take them downstream. Now his job was over, and he'd want to get back to his home base. But he'd become part of her family.

"When will you be going?" she asked.

"Not for a few days, anyway," he said. "I need to get some land legs, and I'll help take the boat apart."

CHAPTER FOURTEEN
Rising Waters

In steady rain the next morning, the men walked the streets of Cincinnati to find a good location for the Millers' house, then they checked at the land office.

"We've found the right place," Father reported at noon. "We'll be living on Sycamore Street. There's a vacant area right on the corner. We can have the entry to our house on one street, and the entry to my surgery on the other."

"What about our house?" George asked.

"We'll get to that after we build the first one," Uncle Paul said.

The rain continued in the afternoon. Betsy's hat and cloak didn't keep her dry as she hurried up the street toward Potter's stable. She wasn't going to ride Silverstreak in this downpour, but she could groom the mare and let her know that she hadn't been deserted. For once George hadn't tagged along. He'd stayed to play with Jefferson on the covered back porch of the inn.

Betsy darted under the porch roofs of the mercantiles as she made her way down the street. The rain pounded down and seemed to gain in intensity. When would it stop?

She didn't stay long at the stable, but talked with Mr. Potter and learned more about the town. She asked about the library, and he told her where it was located. He didn't know the times it was open, but she vowed to find out. She had allowed her books to be stored in the warehouse in the trunk, so there would be one less thing to step around in their small room at the inn, and anyway she'd be able to read other books at the library soon. She'd only retrieved her Bible and writing materials out of the trunk before it was taken to the warehouse.

The rain seemed to have let up when Betsy left the stable and ran from covered porch to covered porch through the shower back to the inn, but soon another storm moved through, dropping buckets of water on the soggy town.

By the next day, Betsy was sick of rain. Was this typical of Cincinnati's weather? Would her new home mean living in constant rain? She sat downstairs in the parlor of the inn and stared out the window. For the moment the rain had turned to drizzle, and ten minutes later she saw sunshine for the first time in days. The street was one continuous mud puddle. The only solid ground, and it was mushy, was in the yards beside the houses where spring grass grew. Even with the rain over, it would take some time for the ground to dry out.

Just then, Marley clomped up the side steps to the inn and barged inside. "River's rising," he announced. "We're watching it, but it could come out of its banks before evening."

"But it stopped raining," Betsy said. "Surely it won't go any higher."

"It's still raining upstream," Marley said, "and that water will flow this way. According to the rain barrel next to the warehouse, we've had over fifteen inches of rain. That's a lot of water. Where's your father?"

"Upstairs. I'll fetch him."

Betsy returned with her father and Uncle Paul and listened to the men talk.

"That warehouse is too close to the river. It could go under. Anything in there that needs moving?" Marley asked.

"My books," Betsy said. "Oh, Father, I left my books in the trunk."

"We'd better move things to higher ground," Father said, "just in case. Let's check around."

Father, Uncle Paul, and Marley left the inn, and Betsy watched until they disappeared from sight. They didn't walk down the muddy street, but stepped gingerly from yard to yard.

An hour later by the grandfather clock in the parlor, they

returned and stood on the front porch.

"Betsy, we're going to need everyone's help to get our movings out of the warehouse. Mr. Potter says we can store things in the stable for the time being. He has a couple of empty stalls. But we can't get a wagon down this muddy street. Get the others." He motioned to his mud-covered feet. "I shouldn't go inside. And tell your mother to wear my old pair of boots."

Betsy quickly climbed the stairs and called to the women. George and Jefferson ran to the front porch from the back porch of the inn. Soon they all traipsed to the river warehouse, single file, finding the most solid footing they could.

"Oh, my," Mother exclaimed as they looked at the Ohio River.

"It's coming up a foot an hour," Marley said, after conferring with some bargemen who had tied up at the public landing.

Jefferson barked, and George trudged into the muddy street to pick up his dog. Jefferson had sunk to his stomach in the mire.

George placed the dog on the flatbed wagon that was stored beside the river warehouse.

"Stay," he said. "I'll get you on the next trip."

It was eight long blocks that sloped upward to Potter's stable, and Betsy made sure she and Mother carried the trunk that held her books. In some places, they couldn't avoid the mud. Her shoes were caked with it, making each step harder. For once she was glad she was wearing her too-short traveling dress that Jefferson had chewed on. It kept the hem from getting so muddy and weighing her down.

They formed an odd parade walking to the stable. Father and Uncle Paul carried two crates between them, balanced one on top of the other. Aunt Eleanor and George carried a trunk, and Marley carried one by himself.

Mr. Potter directed Betsy and Mother to the stall where they deposited the trunk with the books.

"Let's hope the next trunk isn't as heavy," Mother said.

"Silverstreak can help," Betsy said. "That way I can carry the smaller crates on horseback." She saddled the mare and guided her the long, but less muddy, way to the warehouse. Still the horse's hooves were plastered with mud.

Marley handed Betsy two valises. She hooked one over the saddle horn and propped the other in front of her. From his perch on the flatbed wagon, Jefferson barked at the horse as Betsy maneuvered her toward more solid ground.

"Stay." Betsy repeated the order George had given earlier and was amazed that the dog obeyed. Getting stuck in the mud must have made a great impression on him. She glanced at the river. It had taken much less than an hour to get the first load to the stable, yet the water was more than a foot higher than the last time she'd seen it.

Betsy took her load to the stable and returned again.

Other men were at the river warehouse now, carrying stored goods to higher ground. They worked quickly and with little talk.

This time Father helped Betsy load a heavier crate. She secured it with a rope around the saddle horn and balanced it in front of her.

"Just take it as far as the porch at the inn, then return," Father said, an urgency in his voice.

Betsy urged Silverstreak forward. She passed Mother and Aunt Eleanor carrying the headboard of Grandmother's bed between them. George struggled up the porch steps with a large basket, then he headed back while Betsy deposited her load.

By her fifth load to the porch, the river roared only inches below its banks. As George helped Betsy stack her crate on the porch, someone on the street cried, "She's out of her banks!"

That was impossible. How could it rise so fast?

George dropped his end of the crate and yelled, "Jefferson!" He turned and ran toward the river, his shoes throwing mud behind him.

Betsy climbed on the mare and followed him. She pulled up Silverstreak when she saw the river. How had this happened so fast?

Water gushed around the wheels of the flatbed wagon where Jefferson sat howling. George dashed into the waist-high water, which knocked him off his feet and carried him downstream a good ten yards before he regained his footing and waded out of the floodwater. Looking like a drowned rat, he ran to Betsy.

"Help me get Jefferson!" he pleaded. "You're tall, so the water won't be so high on you."

Betsy glanced around. Where were her parents? Too far down the street to help now. She urged Silverstreak through the water, but the mare shied and reared. Quickly she dismounted and tied one end of the rope that she'd used to secure the crates around her waist and the other to the saddle horn.

"You're going to have to mount Silverstreak," she told George.

"I can't," he said.

"You have to. Jefferson's depending on you."

George took a deep breath, put his foot high in the stirrup, and swung into the saddle.

"Now, pull on the reins if I need you to back her up and pull me out of the water," Betsy ordered. She stepped into the raging floodwaters and felt the rush of the water against her legs. With great determination she took one step after another until she reached the wagon.

She climbed up on the wheel and reached for Jefferson. The dog backed away from her.

"Tell your dog to come here," she called to George.

"Betsy!" Father yelled from a block away.

"Jefferson, go to Betsy," George shouted.

The dog inched toward her. When he was in reach, she grabbed for the muddy creature and cradled him in her arms. Now to get down from her precarious perch on the wagon wheel. She felt the wagon lurch under her feet, and with a quick prayer for courage, she plunged into the water.

This time she went under, and in the brief moment that she was submerged, she relived her earlier nightmare of being in the murky Ohio. She fought her way to a standing position and made sure Jefferson's head was out of the water. A glance at the edge of the floodwater assured her that George still sat in the saddle. Father stood behind Silverstreak. Mother and Aunt Eleanor stood at a distance, their eyes opened in horror.

"Hurry, Betsy," Mother called. Betsy stepped staunchly away from the wagon and into the torrent. She immediately lost her footing and went under again. The rope pulled at her waist, and quickly she was back on top of the churning water.

She moved toward the edge of the water, half swimming, half walking.

Step by step Silverstreak moved back, keeping the rope taut between them. Jefferson didn't move in her arms. She glanced down and saw his eyes frozen in fear. They probably matched her own. Six more steps, five, four. Each step became easier as the water became shallower. Three, two, one. She stepped out of the water and into the mud.

She shivered as George climbed down from Silverstreak and grabbed Jefferson. Father hugged Betsy and led her away from the rushing water that was now encroaching on the area where they stood. The dog barked and licked George's face. Silverstreak whinnied, and Betsy leaned on her as they moved farther up the street, out of the water's reach.

"Let's get you to the inn," Mother said. "Whatever possessed you to go out into that torrent?"

"I had to. Jefferson was trapped," Betsy said through chattering teeth.

"Look," George cried. She turned and watched as the floodwaters washed over the wagon and carried it downstream. She shook, not from the wet and cold, but from fear.

Father supported her on one side and Mother on the other as they made their way to the inn.

"Silverstreak?" Betsy asked.

"Your uncle Paul's taking her to the stable," Father said.

"Our movings?" she asked.

"All safely out of the warehouse," Mother said. Aunt Eleanor hustled George and Jefferson along the street beside them.

Two hours later Betsy was warm and dry again. She sat

with George and Jefferson on the front porch of the inn. Their parents and Marley had moved the rest of their belongings from the porch to Potter's stable. The sun was still shining, the rain was over, but floodwaters continued to rise. The adults were helping other townspeople move their belongings to higher ground.

"Marley said the river should crest sometime in the night," George told her. "But it won't get up here."

"That's good."

"Betsy, thanks for saving Jefferson. I don't know what I'd do without my dog. It's a good thing you're so tall, so you could go in after him."

Betsy stared at the house across the street for a full minute, then turned to George. "If you think it's a good thing I'm tall, why do you always tease me about my height? How's the weather up there?" she mimicked.

"No reason. Something to say, I guess. Get a rise out of you."

"Don't do it anymore."

"All right, if it bothers you," he said.

"That's it? You won't do it anymore?"

"No. You're so quiet, Betsy. You should have told me before that it bothered you. It bothered me that you asked if I was afraid of horses in front of those boys at the stable."

"I didn't mean to embarrass you, and I felt terrible afterward. I think we should treat each other the way we want to be treated."

"You mean like the Golden Rule says?" George asked.

"Exactly. George, why are you afraid of horses?"

"They're so big." He looked at the floor of the porch

instead of at her. "I rode Jacob Baker's horse back in Boston, and it threw me off. I've never been back on one until today."

"Silverstreak's big, but she didn't throw you," Betsy said. "Sometimes you have to face your fears. If you want, I'll teach you to ride. Then you won't be afraid anymore."

"Thanks, Betsy. I'd like that," George said.

"I'm going inside," Betsy said. She left Jefferson and George and climbed the stairs to the Millers' room. With quill pen in hand, she sat at a small table and reflected on her conversation with George. Then she began her letter to her friend in Boston:

Dear Mary,
    We are home. Our eventful journey has left its mark on me. I'm not as shy as I was. And George and I have declared a truce. We may even be friends.

There's More!

The American Adventure continues with *Earthquake in Cincinnati*. George Lankford is fascinated by the *New Orleans,* the first steamboat to make it down the Ohio River to Cincinnati.

George is determined to create his own steam-powered engine, but he can't seem to make it work without the help of Charles Lidell, a boy who, as a toddler, was horribly scarred by an overturned pot of boiling water. George appreciates Charles's help, but he's embarrassed by his friend's appearance and the teasing other kids direct at him when he's with Charles.

Then calamity strikes when an earthquake hits Cincinnati, and George's world will never be the same.